The Life & Times of

Christopher Le Monte

By Rocky Russell

Another Okiehayseed Production

The Life & Times of
Christopher Le Monte

ISBN Hardback: 978-1-77419-069-2
Paperback: 978-1-77419-073-9
Ebook: 978-1-77419-074-6

MAPLE LEAF PUBLISHING INC.
3rd Floor 4915 54 St Red Deer,
Alberta T4N 2G7 Canada
General Inquiries & Customer Service
Phone: 1-(403)-356-0255
Toll Free: 1-(888)-498-9380
Email: info@mapleleafpublishinginc.com

Louisiana in the summer time is a very hot and sticky place to be, especially if you are trying to work out in the sunshine. An old man by the name of (Bood-row) Boudreo Le Monte was moving slowly along the rows of cotton as he hoed the weeds that grew there. His ragged white shirt was stained yellow from his perspiration, as were his overalls. His foot ware consisted of a pair of worn out old sandals and he wore no socks. The stickers he occasionally encountered were painful when they penetrated his tough hide. His straw hat was jagged; a few holes were letting the sun to shine onto his gray curly hair. He wanted to quit and go set in the shade of a nearby big oak tree, but if he didn't work a full day he wouldn't have enough money to feed his wife and young daughter that night. The four dollars the farmer had promised to pay him for weeding the cotton patch, these last four days, would feed him and the two women for three, maybe four days. All too soon, he would have to find additional employment.

Lucinda, his young daughter of sixteen was not married. However she was pregnant; due to being raped by a very wealthy land owner, Colonel Gregory Weston, who lived down the road two and a half miles from the house where he and his family lived. Because Colonel Weston was well connected politically, plus very wealthy and they were just dirt poor Cajuns, the law would not do a thing to help them. When Boudreo protested to the parish sheriff, he was thrown out of the court house and told to never return.

Doctor Mitchell was a kind hearted soul, if your skin was the right color, who said he wouldn't charge more than five dollars to deliver the baby when it was time. The doctor was in his late fifties and his health was beginning to fade. "It might as well be a million," Boudreo told the doctor "cause where's a poor man like me gonna find that much money?"

"That's the best I can do," said Doctor Mitchell "If I don't get paid then how can I feed me and mine?"

Lucinda's mother, Sara Jane, said "well . . . I guess we will just have to let a midwife bring that child into da world."

"How much dat' gonna cost?" asked Boudreo.

"Marquette says we can work out her two dollars," was the answer.

"But the real problem is how we gonna feed the youngin' any how?"

"Lord only knows."

A few weeks latter the baby was born. It was a boy. He was on the small side of tiny. Marquette said "That young-un' not gonna live very long cause he be too little, he just be a runt."

Lucinda was a good mother to the child and the boy managed to live through the rough days. Then one day she took the infant to the house of Colonel Weston. She was met in front of the house some distance from the steps leading up to the wide veranda, where the Westons were seated in the shade being waited on 'hand and foot,' so to speak. The lord of the manor saw her coming up the road and went to meet with her before she would be able to reach the house.

"What do you want here?" he growled at her.

"I thought by now you would want to see your son," she said in a nasty tone.

"That's not my son . . . my sons are on the porch . . . so you get your bastard out of here . . . or I'll send for the law."

"Don't you want to know what he looks like?" she held him up with his face uncovered.

"Get out of here," he said loudly.

"Take a good look . . . you sum bitch . . . cause he's gonna' die . . . cause I just can't feed him enough," she began to cry. "If you can't help me than less ways help your son."

He looked at the very small child in her arms. The features of the child reminded him of when his two legitimate sons, when they were that small. "I can't," he said.

"You can't . . . or you won't," she yelled.

"I can't . . . it would break up my marriage," he said.

"What's the death of your son going to do to your marriage?"

"That's a very good question," said the woman coming up the road from the house, Gregory Weston's wife, Barbara.

"This doesn't concern you," he said loudly.

"The hell it don't, you bastard," she said louder "What are you trying to do . . . have children by the whole female population?"

"Barbara please go back to the house and let me handle this," he demanded.

"Like hell I will . . . I demand to see the child you and this . . . woman had together."

"Barbara," he screamed and stepped in front of his wife "go back to the house, now." She pushed past him and quickly came to face Lucinda and the baby. "Awe . . . he's cute," she purred. Just then she was grabbed from behind and spun around. His fist struck her on the chin and she was knocked to the ground unconscious.

"I warned you," he said as he stood over his wife lying on the ground. "Now see what you made me do," he yelled at Lucinda "get the hell out of here . . . right now." His face was red and his blood veins were bulging about his face and neck. Fearing for what he might do next, she turned and ran as fast as her legs could carry her, clutching the infant to her body.

He watched her for a few seconds then he reached down and picked up his wife from the drive way. He quickly carried her into the house where one of the servants opened the double doors. He entered the house with out a word, crossed the wide large living room, and then up the wide curved stair case to their bedroom. There he placed her on the bed by just tossing her onto it. He went to the closet and took out his hat and riding crop. He called to the stableman out the window of the second floor "Get my horse ready and bring him to the front."

"Ya sir," was the answer from the elderly dark skinned man. He went into the stable and soon appeared leading a very fine animal with an English saddle and hurried around to the front of the house.

"It's about time," growled Gregory. "I think I better get me a new groom, you're getting slower every day." He snatched the reins from the groom's hands and led the horse to a set of steps which served to elevate his body. This allowed him to just step across the saddle with out any effort in mounting. He quickly slapped the riding crop onto the animal's side and the wanted results was achieved, as the horse dug his hoofs in and sped away at a high rate of speed.

"It be plain as da nose on yo' face," the groom said to one of the other servants "who's the real bastard around here."

"Sho nuff."

§

"I want that piece of trash and her family, run out of this Parish," he yelled at the sheriff seated behind his desk in the parish court house.

"Simmer down," the sheriff said "the only thing you need to do now is get the judge to place some kind of an order on them to stay away from you and your family."

"You mean a 'Restraining Order' . . . what good would that do? She came right up to the house with her brat. Waving him in front of Barbara's face . . . it was like waving a red flag at a mad bull. Now the wife's all upset."

"I sympathize with you . . . but you have a good Lawyer . . . and the judge is your first cousin . . . so let them handle it for you . . . but what ever you do . . . don't you use any kind of force on those people . . . you hear."

"I just want them to stay away," he said as he exited out the door.

"I pity the women in his life," said the sheriff under his breath.

§

"What's going on in here?" demanded Gregory Weston as he came into the master bedroom.

"I'm leaving . . . you son-of-a-bitch," she screamed at him "I have had it with your rotten temper . . . and this time you have gone two far . . . I am not a punching bag for you to take out your frustration on . . . so it's goodbye."

He came across the room and grabbed her by the arms just above the wrists. "You can't leave me . . . I won't let you."

"Just try and stop me," she screamed in his face. His fist connected to her chin once more and she fell to the floor, but this time still conscious. He dropped to the floor to set on her stomach and pounded her in the face with both fists several times.

"You try to leave me . . . I swear . . . I'll beat you to bloody pulp," he said, and then rose to his feet and walked out of the room.

One of the servants came to her aid. "Oh my . . . yo poor child," she said as she knelt beside her. "Yo needs ta see the doctor right away."

"Help me to my bed . . . please," Barbara groaned.

"Yes um . . . then I gonna send for the doctor." She struggled with her mistress to the bed. Once she was on the bed the maid ran to the window. "Rufus," she called out.

"I's here," said a slender dark skinned lad setting under the large oak tree next to the house.

"Get yo feet to flying and fetch the doctor for Miss Barbara . . . she's done been hurt . . . real bad."

"Yes um . . . I's gone."

§

"You got a broken nose," said the doctor "that's the worst of it. The rest is just bruising which will heal in a few weeks and you'll be good as new."

"I'll never be the same, ever again," she said sternly.

"There's nothing I can do to mend a broken spirit. Medical science hasn't progressed that far, as yet . . . that is still in the hands of the All Mighty."

"Who sent for you?" roared Gregory as he came into the room.

"Your fists broke her nose," said the doctor.

"It wasn't my fists . . . it was that trash dragging her bastard up to my house, trying to claim it was mine. It got Barbara all upset and she was going to leave me."

"Why don't you admit it like a man . . . the child is yours . . . Lord only know how many more there are out there," cried Barbara.

"He is not my child," screamed Gregory.

9

"Colonel . . . I believe the best thing for you to do is to help the child, his mother, and the grandparents. You could give them jobs here on your farm, educate the boy, and in general help raise him," suggested the Doctor.

"What? Bring that trash into my home," yelled Gregory.

"I didn't say you had to bring them into the house . . . you acquired the Mitchell place two years ago, and no one lives there . . . Boudreo could share crop the place for you."

"Why should I do that?"

"It would go a long way in the 'relations department' among the other Cajuns in the area . . . the good will I mean. Don't you see . . . then the others would be more agreeable when dealing with you," explained the doctor.

"I don't know . . . I better discuss this with my Lawyer."

"You do that . . . I think you'll find it will be of great benefit to you later on."

"You do like the doctor says," said Barbara from the bed.

"You made up your mind to stay yet?" he asked harshly.

"Oh, I wouldn't dream of leaving," she said for deep down she was afraid he might just do her in, if she tried to leave. She was from the north while he was a local born and raised man. He inherited all his land and money from his father. He was related to all those with any authority in the parish, so if she was to leave she would need lots of help from afar.

"Colonel . . . there is one last thing I have to say," said the Doctor.

"Yes, what is it?"

"Don't hit your wife again . . . because she's pregnant." He picked up his medicine bag and hat and left the room.

"This true?" he asked her.

"Yes . . . I'm sorry to say . . . it is. Now if you don't mind . . . I want to rest."

§

"I'm sorry," said the sheriff standing on the ground in front of the little shack where Lucinda and her family lived. "This restraining order means that if you go near the home of Colonel Weston, or any member of his family, you will be arrested and put in jail. Is that clear?"

"I just wanted him to see the baby . . . then maybe he'd help him out," she started to cry. "I don't care about me . . . my baby needs help, or he's gonna . . ." the tears begun to flow big time.

"I'm very sorry . . . Lucinda . . . but you can see how it is," said the sheriff and he place the legal document in her hands. Her father came down the steps and held his daughter in his arms. "Boudreo . . . I want to . . . here for the baby," he handed him a five dollar bill. "I wish it was more . . . but I have a family too."

"Thank yo kindly," said Boudreo. "Now you tell that rotten no good sum bitch to keep away from us-ins."

"I'm truly sorry," said the sheriff as he turned to leave. He mounted his horse and rode away.

§

The heat was reaching the ultimate limit of man and beast, but Sara Jane was still working in the field picking the cotton. At a penny a pound she could make as much as three dollars that day, but she would have to keep at it all day. She had started as soon as anyone could see. There had been some twelve men and three women that morning picking the cotton. But as the day wore on they had all turned in their proceeds and retired for the day. However, Sara Jane needed the money very badly to help feed Lucinda's baby. This was one grandmother who was determined they were not going to loose her only grandchild to malnutrition. She tugged at the bag dragging behind her as she placed the puffs of cotton inside. When she could no longer manage to tug it, and fill it with any more cotton, she took it to the wagon. There a man sat in the shade of the tree.

He would take the bag and weigh it, write the figure down on her card and on his tally sheet, then he would dump the load into the wagon. He would then return the long sack to her. And then she would start again to fill it once more.

About three o'clock Sara Jane became ill to her stomach and developed a very bad headache. Things began to swing around as she became dizzier by the minute. "One more row then I'll stop and rest," she said aloud. Suddenly she realized there would never be any more rows to pick. She fell to her knees and said "Lord." She fell forwards on her face to lie still. It was nearly an hour before the man in the shade noticed she was no longer picking cotton. When he could not see her any longer, he thought she had left for the day, so he picked up his things and he left for the house.

It was getting dark when Boudreo began to worry about his wife's not returning from the cotton patch on a neighboring farm. "Lucinda," he called to his daughter inside the shack "I's gonna go see bout yo mama."

"Okay, daddy," she said as she stood in the door way of the house.

Boudreo took the old kerosene lantern and headed off down the road toward the cotton patch. He met some of the other workers from the field that day. When asked about Sara Jane they could only say they had not seen her since noon, or a little later. Fearing the worst he went into the field to search for her. Some time before ten o'clock he found Sara Jane laying face down in the rows of cotton. His screams brought several men with lights out into the field.

§

Sara Jane Le Monte was laid to rest in one corner of a little country church cemetery. Father Andreas conducted the services for the nearly one hundred Cajuns in attendance.

§

One evening, after the lamps were turned off in the shack, someone began calling at the Le Monte domicile. "Boudreo," yelled the man standing at the bottom of the steps to the shack "I would like to talk with you."

"What's ya'll wants this time of night?" he called back while still inside the house. Not knowing the intentions of the man outside, he took his 22 rifle down from the pegs over the door.

"I'm sorry about the hour, but it is urgent that I see you about some share cropping," he replied.

"Who's ya'll?"

"My name is William Gordon . . . I'm an Attorney . . . my client wants you to do some share cropping for him."

"Who's yo client?"

"Boudreo . . . please come out here so I don't have to shout . . . this will only take a few minutes of your time."

The old man returned the rifle to the peg over the door, and then he opened the door. He stepped out onto the squeaky old porch. It had a very bad case of the 'sags.'

"That's better," said the Attorney "My client is making you an offer to do some share cropping on his place . . . if you're interested."

"I's interested fo sho," he said "but who's dis fo."

"My client is Colonel Weston," he said lowly.

"That no good fo nut-in," barked Boudreo as he descended the steps and pointed toward the roadway "yo tell him we's want nut-in from him."

"Boudreo . . . I know how you feel . . . and I'm truly sorry about your loss," said the Lawyer backing up "but please hear me out . . . then if you decided to except then fine . . . and if you don't except then that's fine too. At least I'll have done my job."

"Daddy," called Lucinda from the door way "we needs to hear the fella' what's he got to say."

"Yo sho child?" he asked.

"Yes daddy," she said "on account of the baby."

"Mista yo can says what yo got's to says . . . then yo bess be gone."

"Colonel Weston acquired a sixty acre farm and needs someone to farm it for him. There is a good sound house, barn, good well, a large pond, and it is fenced in so you can run some livestock. There is a good garden area near the house. The Colonel is willing to provide you with all the seed and fertilizer you need, plus feed for your mule from his store in town. In addition he is going to give you credit at his grocery store for the food you and your family will need until the crops are harvested."

"That be nice," Lucinda said "but what about the baby?"

"He'll see to it that the child gets a good education," was the reply.

"That be all?" she asked.

"He is not going to acknowledge the child."

"What dat mean?" asked Boudreo.

"Acknowledge . . . it means he is not going to say the child is his . . . ever."

"I's don't think we's want nary a thing to do with this," said Boudreo.

"Daddy . . . I know I'm no good . . . and you and momma are ashamed of me . . . but we have to think about what is best for my baby," she placed her face into her hands and cried hard. She then turned and ran back into the old shack. Boudreo watched her disappear inside then he started up the steps.

"Boudreo," called the Attorney as the old man climbed to the top of the steps and onto the porch. "What do I tell the Colonel?"

"We's gonna have to think on it some . . . maybe in a day, or two we's has da answer."

"I'll leave my card here," he placed in on the porch by wedging it between the cracks of the decaying deck boards. "My office is in Baton Rouge."

"We's let ya know."

§

"Where's the mother of my husband's baby?" Barbara asked Boudreo. She had driven up in a buggy drawn by a very fine horse which she pulled to a stop a few feet from the steps to the shack.

"Miss Barbara . . . yo aught not to come yere . . . what's yo man gonna say?"

"I don't give a damn!" she said.

"Why Miss Barbara," exclaimed Boudreo.

"I came to see Lucinda and the baby," she said "now where is she?"

"She be in the house," he replied.

"Will you please, help me down?" she asked as she rose from the seat. The horse moved forward just then and she fell back into the seat. Boudreo went to the horse and took the halter rope and tied it to the hitching post. He then returned to help her down to the ground. Her feet no sooner touched the ground then she quickly ran up the steps and then across the porch to stand next to the door.

"Miss Barbara . . . yo aught not go's in there . . . cause it taint no fit place for a lady such as yo self," called Boudreo trying to catch up to her. She waited at the dilapidated screen door and turned her head toward him. When he reached the door he took hold of the door knob and then hesitated. "Ya sho yo wants ta go inside?"

"Yes, Boudreo . . . I must see Lucinda and the baby."

"Yes um," he said then he opened the door. She entered the old shack and went to stand in the middle of the room. The old house was one long room with a home made curtain across one end. It was made from an old wagon canvas and it did provided some privacy to those behind it. At the other end of the room was Lucinda setting on her bed nursing the baby. She closed her blouse and placed the baby back in the wooden crate she used as a crib for the child.

"What's you want with me?" asked Lucinda as she came to the home made table and benches. She motioned for Barbara to take a seat. Lucinda slid onto the bench across from Barbara and brushed at her hair with her hands.

"Child . . . I understand . . . my husband is the father of your child," she said.

"True," she said "he raped me down at te swimmin' hole on the bayou."

"I didn't come here to make trouble for you, or your father," said Barbara.

"What fo then?" Boudreo asked as he took a seat next to his daughter.

"My husband has made you an offer to share crop the old Mitchell place," she said.

"True," said Boudreo.

"It's important to me that you to take him up on his offer," She said.

"Why's dat po-tant ta yo?" asked Boudreo.

"I'm going to leave him one of these days," she said "in the mean time I want to make his life a living hell. You will be very close to our house there and you can help me get it done."

"Miss Barbara . . . what's yo askin' . . . mos' likely be a danger ta yo an' Lucinda," said Boudreo "special if-in da Colonel finds out what yo two is up' ta."

"I know," she said with a smile "but wouldn't it be fun to dig the spurs into that old war horse." She giggled then Lucinda joined in too. Boudreo looked at both of them and frowned. His eyes went wide as Barbara with drew, from her purse, a roll of money and commenced to peal off a few dollars. "Lucinda . . . you take this money and buy what ever the baby needs. She handed the bills to Lucinda. "What the hell might as well buy something for yourself too," she handed her a few more dollars from the collection of bill. "Now don't you worry about a thing . . . the child may not be mine . . . but from now on I'm going to be his fairy god mother." She laughed out loud and so did the others. "Oh by the way . . . what's his name?"

"Christopher," his mother said "after Saint Christopher."

"He's the Patron Saint of travelers . . . why him?"

"Cause my baby one day is going to travel far . . . see places . . . and do mighty good thing for people . . . far, far away from this hell hole."

"I believe you're right," said Barbara as she rose from the table and went to see the child lying in the fruit crate turned into a crib. "Awe . . . he's just adorable." She then turned to leave. "You folks take the Colonel's offer to share crop, now, you hear." She quickly made her way to the buggy. Boudreo untied the animal and she waved as she drove off down the road toward home.

"Honey child," he said with a smile "yo gets dat child an' we's gonna ta Baton Rouge ta gets him a few things . . . yo too."

"Daddy . . . we got to be careful where we spend this money . . . else the Colonel gonna find out."

"Baton Rouge be a mighty big town," he said with a big grin "an' he not owns it all."

§

"Daddy this farm is really a nice place," Lucinda said as they drove the old wagon up the road leading to the house. In the wagon were all of the meager earthly possessions they had. She held Chris in her arms. "Oh Daddy just look at that house . . . why it must have four . . . five rooms at least," she squealed.

"Dat be nice," he said "but look child at dat barn . . . ol' Joker's gonna has a roof over his head fer a change."

"Daddy you aught to get a new mule . . . ol' Joker is really getting old now."

"I's wist I's could child . . . but dat takes money."

"I'll speak to Miss Barbara about that the next time I sees her," Lucinda said. Boudreo stopped the wagon at the gate to the make shift fence that surrounded the house. It was designed, more or less, to keep out the live stock; however it was sorely in need of replacing, the entire length of it. The gate was open so they just past right through when their feet reached the ground. Lucinda ran clutching the baby, right up to the top of the stairs. She paused and stomped on the decking. "It's sound as a dollar."

"Dat be nice," said Boudreo as he started up the steps. She opened the front door and stepped inside.

"Oh Daddy," she squealed "you got-ta see this living room . . . it's as big as our old house."

"Sho nuf," he said as he entered the house. "Most ways it be bigger fo sho."

She ran though the entire house owing and awing at the nice new house they would now call their home. She had her own room with the baby's room right next to hers on the second floor. Boudreo made his bedroom on the main floor in a little side room off the kitchen. Once they had moved their meager possessions inside their new home, it still looked empty.

"I's guessin we-ins need mo things what to fill'er up with," said Boudreo.

"It'll come Daddy . . . in due time, it will come," she said "I just wish momma could have seen it come to pass." She wiped at the tears in her eyes.

"Me too, honey child, me too."

Barbara drove up in her buggy the next day for a visit. "How are you two getting along?" she asked as she pulled up to the house. They were on the front porch and Boudreo went to help her out of the buggy.

"Miss Barbara . . . nice to sees ya again," he said.

"How's little Chris?" she asked as she climbed the steps.

"Growing like a weed," said Lucinda.

"May I hold him?" she asked.

"Don't know why not." She handed him over to Barbara.

"Well now . . . look at this handsome young fellow," she said.

"Miss Barbara . . . there is something I wants to ask you," said Lucinda.

"What is it dear?"

"Our mule, ol' Joker, he's getting old and Daddy needs a new one."

"No, I can't do that," she said. Looking around to face Boudreo "but what I can do is to get you a team of mules and a new plow. It's only right that you have a very good team . . . if you are to make this place pay."

"Miss Barbara . . . I's no got the words . . . thank ya kindly."

"Don't thank me . . . that no good son of a . . . he's going to pay and pay dearly," she growled.

§

So the Le Monte's had a patron saint living in the house of their worst enemy. Barbara delivered a boy early the next year. The two boys were to play together as they grew. Beginning at the ripe age of five and six they were taught by a tutor in the home of the Westons, as well as the local parochial school. The Colonel decided to have Christopher trained to be a butler when he was ten years old. So from that day forth he was in the house of the Westons, any time he wasn't in school. The two older sons of the Colonel had been sent to a military academy when they reached the age of ten. Robert Lee, Barbara's son, and Chris were the only two boys in the house from that day forth.

Boudreo and Lucinda worked the farm and life greatly improved for them. Each year they had a little money extra to save for the future. Boudreo began to feel the years creeping up on him. "Getting old is pure hell," is what the older generation had always said and now for him it was beginning to come true.

Chris was thirteen, when Boudreo took to his sick bed. The doctor came and examined him, and then gave him some pills to take. "It would be best if you would take it easy from now on Boudreo . . . on account of your heart. It doesn't sound good . . . and you need to rest for a while."

"I's got a farm ta work," he said "I's can't be in bed at day time."

"Daddy . . . you heard what the doctor has said . . . so you rest for a few days . . . and I'll take care of things."

"Just a day . . . then I's be rat back to work." Despite the protests of Lucinda Boudreo went back to working the farm. It was a month later as he was picking cotton in the fields, the day was very hot and the sun beat down from a cloudless sky. Late in the afternoon he began to feel dizzy as he pulled the long sack along. He stopped to wipe his brow. "Maybe I's need a drink." He took the loop of the cotton sack from off his shoulder and dropped it to the ground. His steps were uneven as he strolled toward the shade tree where his jug of water had been left earlier that day. The closer he got to the tree the more disarranged his steps became. About ten yards from the tree he stopped to steady himself. He removed his hat and wiped at the sweat on his brow. He looked skyward and said "Sarah Jane honey . . . I's comin." He dropped his hat and slowly twisted around to fall onto his back. The other hands in the field on the next farm saw him fall and they quickly ran to his side.

§

"Christopher," said Father Andreas "I have some bad news for you, my son."

Chris looked him in the eyes for a few seconds "It's my grandfather."

"Yes, it is," said the elderly Priest "He has gone to be with your grandmother."

Boudreo Le Monte was laid to rest next to his wife in a corner of the cemetery at the little country church, with a hundred Cajuns in attendance.

§

"Boudreo Le Monte has past away," said the Lawyer William Gordon to Colonel Weston.

"The old man was making me lots of money from that farm . . .damn it . . .now I'll have to find me some other fool to farm that place."

"What are you going to do about Lucinda and the boy?"

"The boy can stay in my house . . . he'll make a very good butler one day."

"And his mother?"

"Who cares?"

"Colonel, if she leaves, she'll take the boy with her."

"Yeah . . . well then . . . maybe I could use another servant in my house."

§

After the funeral the Colonel came to the farm. Several people were gathered at the house. They were either friends, or a few distant relatives of Boudreo's.

The Colonel rode up on his horse. The animal would not stand still, so he jumped down, and then he struck the horse twice in the face with his riding crop.

"Lucinda," he yelled loudly. She was in the house with a few of the women. When she heard him calling, she came to the porch and stood at the top of the steps. "I'll have a new share cropper here tomorrow . . . so you have to get out."

"What about the crops my Daddy planted . . . they're ready to harvest," she said loudly.

"That's just too bad," he said with a smirk on his face. The people there began to show their disapproval by voicing it loudly. "I own the ground they are planted in and my agreement was with Boudreo . . . but he is gone now . . . so you'll just have to get out."

"Where am I to go?" she yelled.

"It doesn't matter to me," he yelled back "just go." He mounted his horse, the animal tried to gallop away, but he pulled him into a tight circle. "If you want . . . there is an opening for a servant in my house. That way you and the boy can stay there."

"And if I don't want to be your servant?"

"Then you can go to hell, for all I care." He spurred the animal to a full gallop as he rode away. All the people present were sending multiple insults after him.

§

"Miss Barbara there is no way I can stay in the same house with that man," Lucinda cried "I'm taking Chris and leaving."

"Lucinda, get a hold of yourself," she said "I will make him pay for this just like all the other rotten things he has done. He won't get away with it . . . that I promise you."

"I can't . . . it won't work," she cried.

"You take the position and I'll take care of him," she promised. "Besides, now we can be closer together and help each other." She smiled then added "Now we can both make life miserable for the old goat." They both laughed.

As time went by Lucinda became accustomed to being a maid, dishwasher, laundress, cook, floor scrubber and any other dirty job the Colonel could find to add to her misery. Barbara kept her promise and the two women made life uncomfortable for the Colonel, that is, anytime he was at home.

One day the Colonel came into the house drunk and screamed "Barbara . . . what the hell have you been doing with the money in our account?"

"It takes money to run this house hold," she said with a shaky voice. She feared he had found out she had been transferring money to another bank. So when she did leave him, she would have ample funds to live on.

"You have taken over forty thousand dollars out of our account," he screamed "now I know it don't take that much to run this house. So what did you do with it?"

Lucinda was not in the house at the time, she was at the market with Chris shopping for new clothes for the lad. When they returned the Colonel started to scream at her.

"Where did you get the money to purchase clothes for Christopher?"

"Miss Barbara wanted him to have some new ones, cause he's growing so fast."

"Now I know where you have been getting money for all the nice clothes you wear. Barbara has been giving you money all along hasn't she? Or have you just been stealing it."

"You ask Miss Barbara," she said as she backed up to get some distance between them.

"She's not here . . . she's gone . . . for good," he said as he approached her. She looked around for a way to safety. He grabbed her by the arm and struck her with his fist and she was knocked unconscious. An hour later she regained her composure and went in search of Barbara. She was not to be found in the house, stables, barn or any other place. That night she waited for her to come home. Even the next day she wondered where her mistress could be.

The Colonel had all of Barbara's clothing and personal effects packed in trunks and removed from the house. He said they were taken to the train station in Baton Rouge and placed aboard a train.

Two days later when none of the other servants were present, she demanded from the Colonel "Where's Miss Barbara?"

"She's at the bottom of the swamp," he said with a chuckle "you give me any more trouble and that's where you'll be too." He then laughed an eerie laugh.

A cold shiver proceeded up Lucinda's spine. She knew no one would believe her if she was to repeat what he said, so she kept quiet. The Colonel, when anyone asked about his wife, would tell them, she had run away with another man. Everyone knew he was a rather distasteful fellow, so they thought no more about it. Then again, those in authority in the parish were either his relatives, or on his payroll, so none of them were going to investigate her disappearance. In the meantime the Colonel hired another woman to run the house hold. This was a kindly woman, but very strict in the way she wanted things done. Her name was Dolly Motts.

Robert Lee was given a party on his fourteenth birthday. The Colonel was making with the merriment and had been drinking heavily. He said out loud "I love giving my son a party for his birthday."

Lucinda, helping with the festivities, when she overheard his words said "You never gave your other son a party for his birthdays."

The Colonel rose from his chair and ran across the floor to grab her by the hair of her head and dragged her into the next room. He slammed the door shut and threw her onto the floor. He locked the door and tossed the key across the room. She jumped to her feet and desperately tried to find a way of escape, but this room, his study, had only the one door; being an inside room it had no windows. She was now trapped with a mad man at her throat.

"You bitch," he yelled. His fists went into action as he pounded her face and body. Blow after blow she received as he beat her with out mercy. When she fell, he would pick her up and beat her some more until she fell again. Each time he would reach down, grab her, and jerk her up, only to knock her down again.

The other guest decided the party was over and everyone quickly withdrew from the house and out into the front yard. Most of them started for their homes. Dolly ran to the locked door, when she could not turn the knob, she beat on the door with her fists. "Let me in," she screamed.

One of the party guests was a doctor's son and he had been accompanied to the party by his father. The Physician now sprang forward trying to get the door open. "Stand Back," he shouted at Dolly. She stepped aside and he threw himself against the door. When it didn't budge the first time, he hit it again, but it still would not open. On the third try the door jamb split in the lock mortise and the door flew open.

The Colonel was throwing another series of blows when the Doctor and Dolly came to Lucinda's aid. The doctor pulled him away from her limp body laying on one of the tables in the room. The Colonel jerked himself away from the physician and crossed the other side of the room. The medical man now turned his attention to the injured woman. Colonel Weston went to the liquor cabinet near his desk and poured himself a tall glass of bourbon then drank it down in one gulp, only to pour another and repeat the process.

Chris came into the room to see about his mother. He stood beside the doctor as he worked with her. Soon the physician ceased what he was trying to do and cursed under his breath. He took the towel he had been using and covered the woman's face. He looked up into the eyes of the young man standing beside him. "I'm sorry Chris . . . she gone."

Chris stood there looking at her for a few minutes. Dolly came and tried to get him to leave, but he pushed her away and refused to leave. He reached out and took his mother's hand and gently kissed it then laid it across her body. He turned around and slowly walked to the splintered doorway. He stood there looking back at the man who had just taken the life of the last person he rightly could call family. Barbara was gone, as were Chris' grand parents. This man was responsible for the murder of his mother. The rage began to build in his young mind. Who was going to stop this monster?

At his left elbow was a large cabinet where the Colonel kept his guns and knifes. The guns were kept under lock and key, but the knives were displayed behind an unlocked glass door. He selected the large bowie knife and placed it behind his left arm and next to his body to shield it from view of every one in the room. He then moved slowly across the room. When he was at arms length from the Colonel, he moved the knife to his right hand, blade exposed in front of him. Molly saw the knife and screamed "NO CHRIS." The Colonel, looking up and seeing his charge, made a swiping motion with his right hand trying to deflect the large knife, but Chris managed to drive the knife all the way to the hilt into the Colonel's stomach. Chris then turned loose of the handle to leave the weapon lodged where he had just placed it.

The doctor came running when he saw Chris with the knife; however he was too late to prevent the lad from using it. The Colonel looked into the doctor's eyes when he came to his aid. He moaned with the pain. "Pull it out," he said.

"When I pull it out . . . you'll feel a sudden rush in your guts and a few seconds later you'll be dead."

"Leave it in," he screamed "I don't want to die."

"Neither did Lucinda."

"Do something," moaned the Colonel.

"As you wish," the physician took hold of the knife and they looked each other in the eyes for a few seconds. "Goodbye," said the doctor and he jerked the knife free. The Colonel gasped as the knife was withdrawn. He clutched at the wound as he expired. The doctor pushed him back into a chair.

2

"I'm the Parish Prosecutor," said the tall well dress man standing before several men in the jail section of the court house "and there is no way we can get a conviction from a jury." His hand was on Chris's shoulder who was seated in a chair at a table.

"Well what are we going to do then with the lad?" asked the sheriff. "Colonel Weston was a very influential man."

"If we put the lad on trial the jury won't convict him . . . so why even bother."

"Judge Weston wants to hang the lad," said another.

"He can just want . . . but the lad is not going to be put on trial . . . not by me anyway."

"We can't just let him go free . . . not after committing murder . . . and it's the lads own father to boot," roared the sheriff.

"Look at it this way . . . if we put him on trial . . . a jury filled with Colonel Weston sympathizers and they convict him . . . the Cajun's will riot . . . if on the other hand we put even one Cajun on the jury they'll vote to acquit, or it's a hung jury."

"Well we can't just keep him in jail," bellowed the sheriff.

"Just turn him loose," said another man coming into the crowded room.

"Who are you, sir?" asked the sheriff.

"Allen Jackson, Attorney at law," he said "and I represent the lad."

"He killed a man," bellowed the Sheriff.

"I have known the lad and his family for the past sixteen years and I have known the Weston's as well," he said making his way to Chris. He bent down and spoke in the ear of the lad "Let me do all the talking. Don't say a single word . . . you understand?" Chris looked into his eyes and nodded. "In all that time I would have to say, Colonel Weston was not a man at any time . . . a tyrant would be more precise."

"But someone has got to pay for the death of the Colonel," pleaded the sheriff.

"That's right," said Allen "Colonel Weston himself."

"What?" asked the sheriff "How's that?

"I have here in my pocket," he pulled out a folded paper a 'Writ' from Judge Parker . . . his ruling is that the death of Colonel Gregory Weston was justifiable and therefore no one is to be tried in his death." He handed the paper to the sheriff. He then turned to Chris and said "Let's get out of here." They both left the Jail section of the courthouse. A cab was waiting outside which took them a few blocks to the office of Allen Jackson. Once they were inside the office, the attorney said "I have been watching you and this whole mess for several years now, at the request of Barbara Weston."

"You know where she is?" Chris asked.

"No . . . I don't . . . I'm afraid she may be dead," he said lowly "she disappeared shortly after you and your mother went to live in the home of the Weston's. Barbara Weston retained me as her lawyer. She wanted me to handle the transfer of money, from her hands to a bank account in Kansas City. The funds were placed there in the event that she would be able to leave her husband safely. However, she has not, or cannot come forward to claim those funds. She also placed those funds in the name of your mother and yourself. So you're in fine shape . . . money wise that is."

"You mean I can with draw the money Miss Barbara put there?" he asked.

"That's right" it's yours . . . to do with what ever you wish, the only restriction is that you can only with draw one thousand dollars each year, then when you reach the age of twenty one you may take it all out . . . that is . . . if you wish."

"How much is there?"

"Forty Thousand Dollars," he said.

"Some how . . . it don't seem right?"

"Now, about the charges of murder against you . . . Judge Parker's ruling can be over turned by a higher Court. However if you are no longer in the State of Louisiana when it is presented to a higher Court, they will more than likely dismiss it all together."

"So what you are telling me . . . is to leave the State of Louisiana."

"The sooner you leave the better."

"I have to attend mama's funeral . . . then I'll leave."

"You can't take the time. The older sons of Colonel Weston will be here tomorrow," said Allen "They may want revenge, so you better leave now."

§

Chris entered the little country church. He was seeking the priest, Father Andreas, whom he had known all his life. He found the man on his knees before the Alter.

"Father," he said when he was a few feet from the man.

The priest crossed himself and then turned to face the boy. "Christopher, my son, what are you doing here? I thought you were in jail."

"I was until the lawyer Allen Jackson got me set free."

"Free? But for how long? And what are you going to do now?"

"Allen said for me to leave the state before the court can put me on trial."

"What? Just let you go free, if you leave the state? Later they may want you back and then they will put a reward out for you. Then every bounty hunter will be looking for you."

"I came to see my mother and tell her goodbye."

"She is in the side room," said the priest. "The funeral is tomorrow afternoon."

"I can't wait," he explained "Allen said Phillip and Bernie will be here then and they may try to kill me."

"In that case, you may see her." He led the way to a small room near the front of the church. It was bare of any thing fancy, just two chairs, and a long bench beside the lone table. A dozen or more glass candle holders were burning on the table among many more. Two stands were in the middle of the room and they held the lone wooded casket. Chris went to the coffin and stood with his head bowed. The priest slowly raised the lid. His mother was dressed in a white dress and she held a cross with a string of beads in her hands that were folded together. Her face was nearly covered with bandages. Chris stood looking at her for a few minutes. He leaned forward and kissed his mother on her swollen lips.

"Goodbye mother." He turned and went to the table and lit a candle. The priest closed the lid as Chris slowly left the room.

"Where are you going?" asked the priest as they walked to the front doors.

"For now, to Texas . . . later . . . maybe to hell."

"Don't say that my son, don't ever say that again. You have been given a heavy load to bear, but the Lord will see you through it and one day you will enter into his presents. Until then seek the Lord and his forgiveness, my son.

"Goodbye Father,"

"Go with God my child." And he crossed himself.

§

The sun's rays in the early morning hours fell on the back of the young man as he tread along the road way leading toward Texas and freedom. He was weary from walking all day, and the day before. It seems no one wanted to give him a ride. He had slept the night away in a stack of hay just off the road a few yards. He was hoping this day would be the day he received a ride. Sixteen years of age, with no where to go, or anyone ahead waiting for him either, or behind him, he was now the master of his own destiny.

He suddenly heard the hoofs of several horses approaching in the distance behind him. They were coming at a fast pace. His first thoughts were it must be lawmen coming to arrest him again, so he hid in the underbrush at the side of the road. He nervously waited for them to pass. Shortly a man riding one horse and leading five more was hurrying along. Chris stepped out into the roadway again to hold out his thumb for a ride.

"Whoaaaa," said the man on horse back as he pulled his mount to a halt. "Are you a bandit?"

"No Sir," said Chris "I need a ride . . . if you don't mind me riding one of your horses."

"Are you running away from home?"

"I don't have a home . . . anymore."

"Where you bound, young feller?"

"Texas."

"That's so . . . what's in Texas that makes you want to go there?"

"Freedom, sir . . . if I stay in Louisiana the law will put me somewhere I don't want to be."

"Running from the Law are you?" he asked "What ja do?"

"I'm an orphan . . . isn't that enough?"

"That's so . . . well if you want a ride it'll have to be with out a saddle," he untied one of the lead ropes and tossed it to Chris. "That mare is gentle enough for you I guess . . . and she not too fast, so if you were to try stealing her . . . forget it."

"Thanks Mister," said Chris as he tied the end of the rope to the halter to make reins on both sides of her head to guide the mare with. "My name is Chris," he said as he held out his hand. The man reached down and shook hands with him.

"Bucky Morse is my name . . . and I'm wanting to reach Texas some time in the next two days so you better get aboard."

"Yes, Sir," Chris jumped as high as he could to land on his stomach on the mare's back, he quickly swung his right leg over her back and came to a setting position. He scooted into the right spot to set squarely over the mares back for the ride. He no sooner was set then Bucky took off at a fast pace. The mare nearly jumped out from under him. He grabbed a handful of mane to regain his seat on her back. Adjusted his position once more; feeling he was in sync with the stride of his mount he let go of the mane.

Bucky kept the pace up for nearly three hours with out stopping. They rode past houses and people on the roadway, either in wagons, or on horse back. Some were going in the same direction as they, but Bucky would only acknowledge them by tipping his hat to the women folk and giving a sloppy salute to the men. He never stopped to exchange words with anyone.

Chris was beginning to regret climbing aboard this horse bareback. About noon time, Bucky pulled his horse off of the road when they came to a bridge over a little stream of water. He brought them to a halt in the shade of some tall trees.

"We'll rest here for a spell," he announced and dismounted. Chris let out a big sigh as he pulled the mare into the shade and to a halt. He slid down to the ground and nearly fell over. His legs were numb from the ride. With each step he took he would nearly lose his balance, but after a few steps he managed to once more regain the feelings in his legs. "Tie your horse so she can graze a bit." Chris did as he was told "You hungry?"

"Yes, Sir," replied Chris.

"Come over here then." Bucky was opening a pack on the horse he used to carry his supplies. Chris came up to Bucky side. "Here .. . have some jerky and some hardtack," he said handing it to Chris. "It's tough, but it'll fill your innards."

"Thank you, sir," Chris chewed on the jerky for several minutes before he could get a hunk free to chew. "It's tough alright."

"That's so . . . Chris I don't think you'd be running from the law just because you don't want to go to an orphanage . . . so what's the real reason you're running?" Bucky took a seat under a tall Ball Cypress tree at the edge of the stream. Chris found a place in the shade near by.

"I killed a man," he said still chewing on the jerky.

"That's so . . . by damn . . . I'm just a horse thief . . . but you go right to the top on your very first try."

"I killed him because he killed my mother," said Chris firmly.

"Planning on killing anyone else?"

"Not unless they try to kill me first."

"Let me see your weapon," Bucky asked.

"I don't have any," said Chris.

"How are you going to do it then, if someone was to trying to kill you? Are you some kind of a hand to hand specialist?"

"I'll get me a weapon," said Chris "maybe a big knife."

"Really . . . you see that piece of wood there next to you?" Chris nodded "Pick it up . . . now pretend that's a big nasty bowie knife in your hand." Chris took the piece of wood and held it out in front of him and just below his shoulder. Bucky drew a pistol from his belt around his waist and fired one shot. It shattered the piece of wood into several pieces. Chris jumped and stumbled over a little log. He fell to the ground on his backside. "You hurt?" asked Bucky as he watched Chris trying to rise.

"No, sir," said Chris sill shaking from the experience.

"I'll bet you're going to think twice about a knife," said Bucky as he ejected the spent casing from his revolver and placed a new round into the cylinder. He then returned the weapon to the belt of his pants. "Cut your food with a knife or anything else . . . but when it comes to killing a man . . . a good gun is the best thing there is to getting it done . . . and done quickly."

"I see your point," said Chris.

"That's so . . . You water the horses while I catch a few minutes of shut eye. Then we'll be on our way again."

§

"What the hell do you mean you won't prosecute the bastard?" Phillip Weston yelled. He is the oldest son of the late Colonel Weston. He was having a conversation with the district attorney for the Parish.

"Judge Parker signed a writ freeing Christopher Le Monte of all charges," said the district attorney.

"He did . . . did he, well I know how to take care of this matter myself," yelled Phillip as he turned and left the office of the district attorney in the court house. Outside he was met by his younger brother Bernie. "They won't do a thing about it . . . just going to let the little bastard go free after killing our father."

"What are we going to do about it?" asked Bernie.

"We're going to hunt him down and kill him," said Phillip "Dad always said the swamps can hide a world of sins."

"Where do we start?" asked Bernie.

"It's for sure he won't go back to our home," reasoned Phillip "we might catch him at his mother's funeral."

"Right," said Bernie.

§

The services were simple for Lucinda. The undertaker had tried his best, but she was not pleasant to look upon so they kept the casket closed. Only the Cajun's who knew her attended, about a hundred in all. It was held in the little country church house which served the Catholic Cajun's in the rural area of the parish. She was laid to rest along side her parents in one corner of the cemetery on the church grounds. All through the proceedings the two Weston men kept watch outside, hoping to find Christopher Le Monte. When those in attendance began to drift toward home the Weston's became very irritated.

"What are we going to do now?" asked Bernie in anger.

"That Lawyer, who got him off," said Phillip in disgust "we'll just have to pay him a little visit tonight."

§

Allen Jackson was leaving his office late that evening. He was on his way home, when two men grabbed him and dragged him into an alleyway. They knock him out and put a bag over his head, then tied him hand and foot. They loaded him into a waiting wagon and covered him with a tarp. He was then driven out of town and into the country side. He was taken several miles into the swamps to a secluded cabin. There he was revived after being tied in a chair and finally he was allowed to face his captors.

"You men are in serious trouble," he said loudly.

"Mister Allen Jackson … Attorney At Law … you dumb jackass," yelled Phillip in his face "you're the one that's in serious trouble."

"What do you men want? I don't have much money," he sputtered.

"He really is stupid," said Bernie "We're the older sons of Colonel Weston."

"Oh … now I understand," said Allen.

"Do you now . . . well in that case you know exactly what it is we want to know, don't you?" Phillip drew a large knife from his belt and past it under Allen's chin, just a couple of inches away.

"I don't know the whereabouts of Christopher Le Monte at the moment," he said with a shaky voice.

"Oh . . . well now, you better come up with his location . . . real fast like," said Phillip softly while holding the knife near Allen's eyes.

"Look here . . . even if I did know . . . I can't tell you, the communications between an attorney and his client are privileged," pleaded Allen.

"You want to leave here . . . alive?" asked Phillip as he slowly ran his thumb over the sharp edge of the large knife, "then you better un-privilege it real fast."

"I can't . . . I took an oath," pleaded Allen. The sweat began to form on his brow as he watched the knife moving to and fro inches in front of his face.

"Suit your self," said Phillip. He moved the knife slowly in closer to Allen's face. Allen moved his head back as far as he could. "Grab his head." Bernie took hold of Allen's head and held it in an upright position. Phillip placed the tip of the knife against Allen's flesh an inch under his left eye. "Where is the little Bastard?"

"I don't know," shouted Allen.

Phillip pushed the knife forward to just penetrate the hide enough to bring blood. Allen screamed from the pain and then he let loose a few obscenities.

"You gonna tell us now?" asked Bernie.

"I can't," said Allen. He fought at his bonds trying to free his hands.

Phillip placed the knife against his soft flesh on the right side, just under the eye. "Where is he?"

"I don't know," yelled Allen "he left town. I told him to get out of the state as fast as he could."

"Now . . . why would you want to do a thing like that?" asked Phillip.

"Because of what you two might do . . . if you were to find him," said Allen.

"You're right about that," said Bernie "only where did he go?"

"I don't know," said Allen. His voice was quivering. He was nearly in tears, anticipating the knife cutting his flesh once more.

"Now you're lying," said Phillip "you know where he went and you know just how to get in touch with him . . . so now either you tell us what we want to know or, I'll have to do a lot more carving on your face."

"I told you the truth," pleaded Allen.

Phillip pushed the knife forward to cut a small nick in his skin. Allen screamed with the pain. He cursed loudly.

"Shall we try it again," said Phillip "where did he go and how do we find him?"

"I can't tell you what I don't know," screamed Allen.

"I wonder what he'd look like with out his nose?" said Phillip as he placed the knife blade in front of Allen's eyes just above the middle of his nose.

"I saw a man once with out a nose," said Bernie "It was a horrible sight."

"No, no, not that," screamed Allen "please, not that."

"Then tell us," shouted Phillip. He placed the edge of the blade on the center of his nose. Allen shook with fear as Bernie held his head in place.

"Okay, okay . . . your mother set up a bank account in Kansas City so she could leave the Colonel. Chris's name is on the account too," said Allen.

"Our mother?" asked Phillip.

"Barbara, your mother."

"She's not our mother," said Phillip "Lucy was our mother . . . she died when I was six and Bernie was four. Barbara's our stepmother."

"That I didn't know," said Allen "Anyway Barbara opened an account there and placed funds to live on . . . if and when she could get safely away from your father."

"Now you see Bernie, I told you . . . Allen would tell us whatever we want to know."

"He sings real pretty," said Bernie laughingly. They both laughed out loud.

"You're going to let me go now, please I told you everything I know."

"Sure, sure," said Phillip. He held the knife in his right hand and cut the ropes that secured Allen to the chair. He stood and rubbed his wrists to get the blood flowing once more. Taking his handkerchief he wiped at the wounds on his face. "Before you go . . . there is one . . . small minor detail."

"What's that?" asked Allen as he neared the door to the cabin.

"As we see it . . . you helped free a murderer . . . so that makes you his accomplice," reasoned Phillip.

"I'm an Attorney . . . it's my job to defend people," Allen said.

"And it's our job to see to it that our father's killer is punished," said Phillip.

"That's right and anyone who helps him," said Bernie.

Allen suddenly realized, they were not going to let him go free, so he turned to run through the open doorway. Phillip held the knife high over his shoulder and with careful aim threw it with all his might. Allen was less than ten feet outside the door when he felt a sudden over whelming pain in his back. He stood there for a few seconds as his life began to drain away. Then he fell forward to land with his face to the ground.

"What're we going to do with him now?" asked Bernie in near panic, seeing what his brother had just done.

"The swamp . . . dear brother," said Phillip "like daddy always said it can hide a world of sins." They both began to laugh out loud.

§

"What are you two planning to do with Chris . . . if you find him?" asked Robert Lee Weston as the three of them were gathered in the dinning room of their home.

"I plan on slowly slitting his throat," said Phillip as he drew his thumb across his neck.

"Just after we cut off his . . . manhood," said Bernie with a big grin.

"Why are you so set on killing him?" asked Robert.

"You were there . . . he killed our Father . . . so why do you have to ask?" roared Phillip.

"He did it because Father killed his mother," said Robert.

"That bitch . . . she was a no good Cajun," said Bernie.

"It doesn't matter," screamed Phillip "the fact is he murdered our Father."

"But Father . . ." Robert was cut off.

"Our Father," roared Phillip as he got right in Robert's face "not yours."

"He was married to my mother," yelled Robert.

"Yeah . . . but she was just a whore and she liked Cajun men . . . any one of them," said Bernie.

"So as you can imagine . . . its any body's guess as to which one of those low down Cajuns is your father."

"You take that back," screamed Robert.

"I don't have to take anything back," roared Phillip "you get out of this house and stay out."

"This is my home too," pleaded Robert.

"Not any more," said Bernie "in fact if you're not gone in one minute," he held up his watch "we'll do some carving on your sorry hide, too."

"This is not fair," sobbed Robert.

"If you're still here when the time is up," said Phillip as he drew his Bowie knife "you can join your whore of a mother in the swamps." The two laughed as Robert began to cry. They both took steps toward him and he turned and ran for the door of the house. He didn't stop running until he was several yards up the road leading away from the house. He was all out of breath from running so hard. He stopped to rest in the shade of a tall oak tree. He looked around for some kind of reprieve from this predicament in which he found himself.

"Them brother's o' yern will kill you fo sho," said a tall thin man which served as the stableman on the Weston Plantation.

"They can't do this to me," said Robert.

"Sho looks like they's can," the man said. "Yo' best's be leavin' this place."

"Where can I go?" he asked with eyes filled with tears and his soul filled with fear.

"Yo' best's go see the Padre at the Church."

§

Robert waked all that afternoon to the little country church where Boudreo, Sarah Jane, and Lucinda were buried. Robert found no one there so he started walking into Baton Rouge some twelve miles further on down the road. At a fork in the road, he took to the right. This road would by pass the city, but it would take him to the Monastery where the Padres lived. That evening just after dark he came to the gate of the Monastery. He entered the little entry way and rang the bell for someone to allow him to enter.

"May I be of assistance to you, my child?" asked an elderly Monk.

"I wish to see Father Andreas," replied Robert.

"Whom shall I say wants to see him?"

"Robert Weston."

"I will get him . . . please wait here," said the Monk and he turned to leave.

"Hurry . . . please," said Robert loudly. He looked around and located a bench to set on and there he placed his tired body. It seemed like hours passed as he waited. Soon the Padre came to the gate.

"Robert . . . my son," said Father Andres as he opened the gate and came to him with out stretched arms. Robert ran to him and they embraced. He began to sob as the man held him closely. "What's this?"

"Phillip and Bernie have kicked me out of the house," he sobbed into the Priest robes. "They called my mother a whore . . . and they threatened to kill me."

40

"I was afraid this might happen," said the priest "you come with me." He led the way inside the compound and across the inner court yard to a long building. He took Robert to an office where another Priest was seated behind a crude desk. He was trying to write a letter by the light of several candles. "This is Robert Weston," said Father Andres "his older brothers have turned on him and expelled him from their home."

"Lord, have mercy," said the man as he crossed himself. "Brother Andres, you know what must be done . . . so get to it." He returned to his writing.

"I will need to leave the Monastery for a short while tonight."

"Yes, yes, whatever you need . . . just do it." The Monk seated at the desk waved his hand with out looking up.

"Robert you will stay in this room," said the priest as he entered a room just down the hall a short distance. "Brother Mitchell will bring you some food and drink."

"What will become of me," he asked with a quivering voice.

"You're not to worry about it . . . just leave every thing to me," he replied "you rest now and I'll see you in the morning."

§

Bucky slept for nearly two hours as Chris took care of the horses. When he woke he sat up and looked all around then at his pocket watch.

"Damn it, boy . . . you let me sleep too long," he roared. He jumped to his feet and grabbed the saddle and went to his horses, there he placed it onto a different mount. Next he took the pack saddle and placed it onto a different horse. "Don't just stand there . . . get a horse and let's hit the road . . . we got a long way to go and a short time to get there."

"Yes, Sir," said Chris as he untied a horse from its mooring. He tied the rope to both sides of the halter and then mounted.

"You like that one . . . do you?"

"I like black horses," said Chris.

"That's so . . . let's ride." he took the lead rope and pulled it to the saddle horn. The other horses followed closely as he rode out of their little rest area and onto the road way. "Texas is that way so we better make tracks."

Chris came up beside Bucky as they rode along. "Would you teach me how to shoot like you do?"

"You want to be a gunfighter do you?" Bucky looked at him in the eye.

"I need to know how to defend myself."

"There are four things to being a good gunfighter."

"That's so," said Chris with a smile on his lips.

"The first is being fast on the draw," said Bucky sternly "Second is being able to hit what you're shooting at."

"Fast and accurate."

"Third is, knowing when to draw and shoot. Most men won't fight . . . they'll back down, or turn tail and run."

"How do you tell when a man wants to fight?" asked Chris.

"His face will change . . . some will bite their lip . . . others will spread their eyes wide . . . and others will go white . . . while others turn red."

"Fast . . . accurate . . . face will change . . . you said there was four. . . so what's the forth?"

Bucky pulled his horse to a halt. He sat real still for a few seconds then he looked Chris in both eyes. "The fourth . . . the most important of all . . . it's that you don't give a damn whether you live or die." There was no smile on his face. "Some say there is a fifth one . . . I'd say it's being willing to kill with out any hesitation. If you're going to pull a gun on someone, don't stop to think about it after you draw, you shoot . . . and shoot to kill." He turned his horse to the west and dug in his spurs.

For the remainder of the day Chris rode behind Bucky some distance away. He thought about what Bucky had said, and then he thought about what was behind him. Would the two brothers chase after him? Then there was their younger brother Robert Lee, would he get involved also? Robert was standing right there when Chris's mother was beaten to death by the Colonel. Robert saw him use the Bowie Knife on the Colonel. Which side would Robert be on if and when it came to a show down? Did Chris, now have two, or would it be three Westons on his trail? Then again what about the law, would they be coming after him as well?

Just before sundown, Bucky pulled the horses off the road way and onto a grassy area some distance from the road. Here he unsaddled the horses and tied them with hobbles on their feet so they could graze, but would not be able to stray very far. Chris gathered fire wood and started to build a fire.

"What the hell you trying to do boy . . . start a forest fire?" roared Bucky when he saw the pile of wood Chris was attempting to light. "First . . . you clear the area of all leaves." He bent down and raked them back. "Then you dig a pit" he pulled out his hunting knife and jabbed it into the ground several times then pulled the dirt up to form a ring around the pit. "Then you place a few dry leaves in the pit and light some others." He struck a match and lit the leaves in his hand. When they were burning rightly enough he place them into the pit, and then placed a few more on top. Next he took some small dry twigs and placed them one at a time at different angles on the burning leaves. When they caught fire he piled larger dry limbs onto the fire. Finally he added a few bigger chunks to the fire. "That's how you do it, boy."

"Back home we just raked up a big pile and set it afire," said Chris.

"That's so . . . where you from . . . the swamps, aren't you, boy?"

"I guess you could say that . . . anyway there seemed to be lots of water all around," said Chris. "There is one thing . . . I would appreciate you not doing."

"What's that?"

"Don't call me 'Boy' again, sir please."

"That's so . . . what you gonna do about it if I do?"

"Nothing . . . on account of you helping me . . . I would just have to leave you and go on by myself."

"That's so . . . in that case, you'll find some bacon and beans in the bag over there . . . and some coffee too . . . you get it out while I get us some water from the stream over there." Chris retrieved the items while Bucky went for the water. When he returned he looked at Chris kneeling by the fire and the items place on a cloth next to him. "Chris . . . just how are you going to cook our supper?" Chris looked down at the items and then realized he had forgotten the cook wares in the other bag. He jumped up and gathered them up. "Looks like you got a lot to learn about living on the trail."

"Bucky . . . I made up my mind," said Chris as they were finishing eating the evening meal.

"That's so," said Bucky.

"I want to be a gunfighter . . . so will you teach me?"

"That's so . . . well I can only teach you so much . . . the rest you will have to learn by yourself."

"Like what?"

"You'll have to study men . . . watch how they react in different situations . . . who will most likely try to kill you and who will want to run when you face up to them."

"I'm young . . . I got lots of time to learn."

"Listen lad, you don't have any more time then me or the next fellow who comes along. You and each of us only have the next breath we take and no more. So if you want to take that next breath . . . You've got to be sure of your adversary . . . fast on the draw . . . accurate with your shots . . . don't care if you live or die . . . and very willing to kill without any hesitation."

"I still want to be a gunfighter," said Chris after taking a few seconds to reflect on Bucky's words. "The way things are right now. . . I guess I don't have any choice."

"That's so," Bucky took a deep breath and held it for a while then let it out slowly "school starts tomorrow . . . you take the first watch," he handed his pocket watch to Chris and said "Wake me at midnight . . . and no sleeping on guard duty."

"What do I watch for?" asked Chris.

"Well, how about anything that could be of a danger to us . . . or to the livestock."

As Bucky slept, Chris would set for a while, and then to ward off sleeping on duty he would walk around for a little while. He kept his eyes on the horses as they grazed nearby. He watched the roadway several yards distant. A few people were traveling now and then on the roadway, even in the dead of night. No one stopped, or acted like they could see the two of them camped in the little clearing in the trees. Just before midnight Bucky rose from his make shift bed.

"I'll take over now," he said and slipped on his boots. "I couldn't get much sleep with you wandering around all over the place.

"I heard you snoring," protested Chris.

"I don't snore," taunted Bucky "see to it that you don't either."

Chris fell into a deep sleep in a very short time. To him it seemed like he had just closed his eyes when he was rousted from his bed by Bucky.

"Get up . . . we got a long way to go today," he said loudly.

"You going to teach me to shoot today?" asked Chris.

"That's so . . . you want breakfast first . . . or just shooting lessons?"

"Breakfast," Chris answered.

"That's so . . . eat up and let's hit the trail," said Bucky. "We'll make a stop in a little town called 'Nugget' to see a gunsmith I know."

Chris quickly ate his food and on the way to his mount he said "We gained a few more horses."

"That's so . . . I managed to locate three more early this morning," said Bucky "that one there has a saddle . . . so you take him today."

"Where did you get them so early in the morning?" Chris asked.

"That's so . . . there's a large ranch near here . . . it has an open barn" said Bucky softly "and didn't I say, I was a horse thief . . . so we better put some distance between us and their owners before they're missed."

Chris rode that day in the comfort of a saddle. About two in the afternoon they reached the Sabine River and crossed over into the State of Texas. Just after three they rode into Nugget, a very small place on the side of the road. Here Bucky turned onto a road leading out of town to the north. About a mile further he came to a large ranch complex. He entered by the main gate with a sign over it that read 'T bar K'. They rode up to the large corral and a cowboy opened the gate for them to enter and then several more cowboys came to the corral. Bucky and Chris dismounted and turned the extra horses loose inside the enclosure.

"Mister Kingston here?" asked Bucky of the cowboys that had gathered around.

"He's in the house," said a rather tall and heavy set cowboy. His clothing was cleaner then the others. "Here he comes." After a few seconds a nicely dressed man came to the corral.

"I say . . . Bucky old chap . . . how do you do?" inquired Mister Kingston with a heavy English accent so strong, sort a like the sent on an onion.

"That's so . . . howdy Mister Kingston," said Bucky stepping through the gate to greet the Gentleman.

"I say . . . I see you brought me some more remounts."

"That's so . . . seven in all . . . good and sound . . . each and every one."

"I say . . . Bucky . . . who's the lad . . . your son perhaps?"

"No, just a hired hand," he touched Chris' shoulder. "You know, to help me in my old age."

"Bucky . . . you're not any older than I am and I get along splendidly."

"That's so . . .have your man look them over . . . this time, give me a good price."

"I say . . . is anyone looking for them?" asked the Englishman.

"Maybe, but not for a week, or more," chuckled Bucky.

"Twenty dollars a head," said the Englishman and his face lost its smile.

"Twenty-five."

"Twenty dollars and not a cent more," said the Englishman sternly.

"That so . . . sold," said Bucky "I can never get you to give anymore than that."

He counted out the money. Bucky put it into a money belt he wore around his waist and Chris's eyes went wide when he saw it. Each compartment was full of bills.

"How much you got in there?" asked Chris.

"Two thousand one hundred and forty five dollars," was the reply "now mount up and let's get you something to shoot with."

§

Their next stop was back in the little town of Nugget where Bucky pulled up in front of a small gunsmith shop. Inside the small building there were lots of guns, some in racks on the walls, others lined up on the back counter, a few lying on the front counter, the new or nice ones arranged under the glass counter, and lots of them plied high on the floor. Any kind of a firearm anyone could have imagined was inside that shop. The owner was a little man not much bigger than Chris.

"Lars Northup," yelled Bucky when he entered the door way.

"Bucky my old friend," He spoke with a Swedish Accent and hurried to shake hands with him. "What's yo got ta have this time?"

"That's so . . . I got a young friend here . . . his name is Christopher Le Monte, and he needs a gun . . . if you can tell us where we might find a gun shop here abouts."

"Lars Northup's Gun Shop is the only one in this here county, by golly" he laughed loudly "So name yo caliber and lay out yo money." He held out his hand to Chris and they shook.

"That's so . . . what you got in thirty eight?" asked Bucky "I want the lad to learn to shoot first with a lighter caliber. When he's able to handle it we'll move him up to a forty five."

"I bet-cha I got just the weapon yo be looking fer," he went to the counter and removed a revolver from the glass case. "This is a Smith and Wesson thirty eight. It's light . . . breaks open at the top and kicks out the spent cartages . . . quick to reload . . . and it has pretty good stopping power to boot."

"That's so . . . how far?" asked Bucky as he inspected the gun.

"What yo shooting at?"

"Rabbits," Bucky winked at Chris.

"Eighty five feet . . . maybe a little more . . . but if it was a man . . . maybe forty feet," the Swede looked sternly into Bucky face.

"That's so . . . how much ammo you got for this thing?" Bucky handed the gun to Chris.

"I got ten boxes of ammo . . . that's . . . five hundred rounds . . . if ya was to save the casings I can reload them for yo . . . save a few dollars that way."

"What you think Chris?"

"Feels good," said Chris with a big smile on his face.

"That so . . . how much?" asked Bucky "and he'll need a belt and holster too."

"Forty dollars," said the gunsmith with a very straight face. There was silence in the room for a few minutes.

"That's so . . . Chris you got forty dollars?"

"In Kansas City," he replied.

"That's so . . . we'll take it . . . and I'll need a box of forty five Colt."

"Bucky, just for yo . . . I throw in two boxes of forty five Colt with the deal."

"That so . . . thanks Lars . . . we'll come to see you when we need something a little bigger."

"Yo do that."

§

Phillip and Berne went to see the sheriff of the parish. "You boys want to do what?" asked the sheriff.

"We want to put up a reward for the capture of Christopher Le Monte," said Phillip.

"You can't do that unless he is wanted by the law," explained the sheriff. "Not until the parish prosecutor tells me otherwise Christopher Le Monte is a free man."

"There is nothing you can do then?" asked Phillip.

"Not a thing."

"We should have known better then to ask you to do anything," said Phillip "looks like all you want to do is wear out the seat of your pants setting behind that desk."

"Talk like that will get you two into a whole lot of trouble," warned the Sheriff.

"Who from, a weak minded moron like you," taunted Bernie.

"That does it," said the sheriff rising from his chair "get the hell out of my office."

"With pleasure," said Bernie "the air's better outside anyway."

Outside the court house Bernie stopped Phillip. "Phil, how are we going to find Chris now?"

"There is no law that says we can't post a reward for information as to the location of Chris," said Phillip.

"How about putting it in the news papers?"

"Good idea . . . let's go see the editor," said Phillip "and stop calling me Phil."

§

Bucky took Chris to a cabin in the woods near the plains of San Jacinto.

"Who lives here?" asked Chris as they drew close to the cabin.

"I do," said Bucky.

"Do you have a wife?" asked Chris.

"Not any more . . . she left me a few years back . . . so it's just me." He pointed to a large fenced area "we'll put the horses in there. You feed and water the horses while I get a fire started to cook some food for our supper."

"Yes sir," replied Chris. "Bucky . . . you think we got time for me to try out this gun?"

"You listen and listen good . . . don't ever be in a hurry when it comes to shooting . . . cause you don't ever want to make a mistake. Once something is shot it's not likely you can ever un-shoot it."

"Yes sir," said Chris. He took the horses to the pen and Bucky carried their supplies into the house. Chris worked the pump to fill the water trough with fresh water for the horses. Then he took a pitchfork and tossed them some hay from the stack in the make shift barn. He went to the house "Where do you keep the saddles?"

"Just put 'em in the barn," said Bucky "hang 'em on the ropes with the loops . . . other wise the rats will chew on 'em."

"Rats . . . you got rats?" asked Chris with a disgusted tone.

"That's so . . . they make good targets," he said with a smile. Chris smiled back and returned to the barn to hang up the saddles.

Chris was up bright and early the next morning. He walked around outside and strolled along the clearing in the woods. The landscape was mostly pine trees, a few oaks and some sweet gums, then with the under growth being so thick he couldn't see very far into them. He turned to face the cabin when he heard the door open and shut.

"You're up already," said Bucky "did you eat anything?"

"Yes sir," said Chris "I ate the leftover bacon and beans . . . and one of those things you call a biscuit."

"That's so . . . Look, if you complain about my cooking . . . then you can do it." They both laughed a little. "You go get your gun and let's start the lessons."

Chris nearly ran to the door of the cabin as he hurried to collect his gun and ammo. Once inside the cabin he opened the cloth bag which held his weapon. He drew out the gun belt and holster. These he place around his waist and pulled the belt tight. He then placed the S&W in the holster. Taking a box of ammo from the sack he hurried to where Bucky was waiting. He looked at Chris for a few minutes.

"You sure you want to be a gunfighter?"

"Yes sir . . . quite sure."

"That's so . . . Alright, listen and listen good, the first thing to remember is . . ."

For the next ten days and sometimes into the nights Chris listened to every word Bucky spoke. He followed his direction to a tee. He practiced and practiced each and every day. At the end of each day Chris would take the gun apart and clean it. Then he would oil and reassemble it once more. He hung the weapon on the bed post at night. Sometimes Bucky would wake him from his sleep during the night and he would act like someone was attacking him. During the day he shot cans, bottles, rocks, pine cones and rats. Bucky even had him shoot things he would toss up into the air. The last day of the lessons Bucky took him into the shade of a large oak tree where Bucky kept some chairs so they could set in the shade during the heat of the day.

"Chris . . . I've taught you everything I know about gun fighting . . . the rest, you'll have to learn on your own. Not all men react the same way in a confrontation, some will run, others will take their time and a few will draw and fire away . . . but then there are those who will not face you . . . they'll try to get behind you and shoot you in the back if they can."

"How do I tell the difference?" pleaded Chris.

"That . . . you'll just have to watch and wait," said Bucky "now don't get yourself into anything you can't handle for a while . . . when you're older and wiser you'll know how to tell them apart."

"Bucky I want to thank you for teaching me this much," said Chris as he held out his hand.

"If you really want to thank me . . . take off that gun and throw it in the water bucket."

"I can't do that," said Chris "Not while there's someone after me."

"That's so . . . Chris stay alive . . . please . . . just stay alive." Bucky rose and walked to the pen with the horses. He took his mount and saddled it. When he rode past Chris he said "I'm going to see someone . . . I'll be back around sunset." He turned his steed to the south and dug his spurs into the animal's side and galloped away. Chris walked back into the house and began taking his gun apart to clean it.

Bucky rode about quarter of a mile away and dismounted. He quickly and very silently returned to the cabin on foot with out his horse. He had spotted something or someone in the brush when he rode away.

"Reach for the sky," yelled Bucky at the man sneaking up on the cabin.

"Bucky," said the man all surprised "don't shoot . . . it's me . . . Choctaw Charlie."

"That's so . . . I knew who you were the minute I laid eyes on your lousy hide," said Bucky.

"Then why'd ya sneak up on me?"

"Cause you're an injun and I just love sneaking up on injuns." Bucky was laughing.

"Very funny," said Charlie "You know I'm a half breed."

"That's so . . . well, I was sneaking up on the injun half. So what brings you to my cabin?" asked Bucky.

"This," he held out a folded page from a newspaper.

"Let's see," Bucky took the paper and unfolded it to stare into a picture of Chris. "Holy Hanna," Bucky hurried to the cabin and inside he found Chris setting at the table cleaning his gun. "You sure are something." He handed the page to Chris.

Chris looked at it for several seconds then laid it down.

"So, they're using the newspapers to find me," he said calmly.

"That's so . . . five hundred dollars will be paid for any information as to the location of one Christopher Le Monte," read Bucky "Boy that's going to bring every bounty hunter in three states looking for you."

"So," said Chris "It didn't say anything about . . . arrest . . . extradition . . . or conviction."

"That's so . . . you show your face in any town around here and you'll be snatched up so fast," warned Bucky "You've got to get away from here. There's no telling how many others saw this newspaper . . . like this renegade." Bucky was pointing to Charlie.

"The paper said he killed his own father," said Charlie loudly "So why are you helping some one like that? Let's just turn him over to the law and collect the money."

"It just so happens, I like the kid," said Bucky after a few moments.

"You're crazy," said Charlie loudly "He's no good, so let's collect the reward."

Chris watched the face of Charlie as he became more agitated as he realized there was no way Bucky was going to help him collect the funds. Chris quickly reassembled his revolver and loaded it. He then placed it in the holster at his side, with the safety strap off. He went and stood next to his bunk.

"Chris you pack some food and we'll head west . . . maybe we'll go to San Antoine . . . I know a ranch near there . . . we can hide out for a few months . . . longer if we have too."

Charlie's face changed as Chris watched. Just like Bucky had said it would. The Indians face became darker by the second. His hand moved slowly toward his knife on his belt. When he pulled the knife Chris sprang into action. His S&W belched fire and lead when he squeezed the trigger. The bullet hit the blade of the knife and the impact sent it flying through the air, which left Charlie with a stinging hand. He gripped it tightly and gritted his teeth from the pain.

"What the hell?" yelled Bucky as he turned to face Chris.

"He was going to stab you in the back," said Chris as he pointed to Charlie.

"He lies," said Charlie in a high pitched voice.

"You're the one who's lying," said Bucky when he saw the knife on the floor. "Chris . . . you should have killed him."

"But I thought he was your friend," said Chris.

"That' so . . . he was . . . but not any more," said Bucky as he moved to his gun belt hanging on the pegs over the head of his bed. He drew out his weapon. "You'll have to go ahead on your own while I stay here."

"You're not coming?"

"That's so . . . I have to stay behind and keep this renegade from leading those half brothers of yours onto your trail. The longer I can keep him here the better your chances will be of getting in the clear." Bucky removed his money belt and took out several bills from one pocket. He took a piece of paper and wrote a short note on it. "You'll need some money and this is where you should go. They're good friends of mine and you'll be safe there. I'll see you kid."

"Thanks for everything," said Chris. He picked up his few possessions and stuffed them into a tote sack. He hurried to the door and out to the horse pasture. He caught his mount and saddled him quickly. He then tied the sack of items behind the saddle and mounted. He dug in his spurs and the horse sped away.

Bucky watched him from the doorway of his cabin. They waved goodbye to each other as Chris rode away, and Chris yelled "So long." When Chris was out of sight, Bucky slowly walked out into the yard. Charlie came to the door of the cabin.

"Damn you Charlie . . . I really liked that kid," said Bucky nearly in tears.

"He's a no good murdering punk," yelled Charlie "we could have split the reward for his worthless hide."

"You know . . . I was just wondering . . . how long a rotten no good half breed can stay alive tied to that tree?" said Bucky as he waved his pistol around and pointed with his other hand to the big oak near the cabin.

"You wouldn't do that?" Charlie said with fear in his voice.

"That's so . . . you sorry son-of-a," he held the word because he knew Charlie's mother to be a very fine person. He then continued "I aught to just shoot your sorry hide full of holes."

§

Chris rode west for several days. His supplies were about all gone. He kept to the woods and gullies during the day time, when he might meet people on the road. When he came to a town, he would circle around and come in from a different direction, and when he left he would leave the same way. He figured if some one spotted him they wouldn't know which way he was traveling.

He kept traveling west, until he came upon a large heard of cattle. They were stretched out for a couple of miles, or more. Cowboys using bull whips rode along on both sides of the cattle. They were, more or less, headed north. He watched for nearly an hour as the herd moved slowly along. In the distance he could see a wagon coming along at a hurried pace. It nearly turned over crossing a small gully. The driver screamed obscenities at the team as they scrambled up the bank of the ditch. Once they were on flat ground again, the driver whipped them up again. Chris rode parallel to the wagon to see if there was going to be a wreck. About six more miles and the driver pulled the wagon to a halt on a piece of high ground. Nearby was an old dead tree which had dropped most of its smaller limbs to the ground. This would serve as their supply of fire wood. The wagon driver quickly unhitched the team and removed their harness. He then went about setting up camp. A young boy gathered some wood for the fire and he soon had a good sized fire burning. The driver and cook hung a large coffee pot on the iron rods over the fire. Then he hung a large cast iron pot over the fire to cook something. Finally he placed a large metal oven on the side of the fire and placed inside some dough balls to make bread.

"You looking for something?" demanded a man behind Chris.

"No sir," said Chris as he razed his hands when he heard the action of a rifle being worked to load a round into the chamber.

The rider came closer, but still behind Chris. "Move on down the hill" he ordered. "We'll just let Mister Morgan figure you out."

"I was only watching," said Chris.

"Shut your mouth and move before I fill your thieving hide full of lead."

"Okay," said Chris and he slowly walked his mount toward the wagon. They were met by two of the cowboys who came to see what the other one had caught.

"What've you got there, Bob?" asked one of the cowboys.

"He's been watching the herd for more-n two hours now," said Bob "I think maybe he be one of them 'stampeders."

"I was just passing through," said Chris "This is the first time I ever saw so many cows." Everyone began to laugh a little.

"He's no stampeder," said a man riding up on a very tired mount. "I've been watching him for the past hour."

"What's a . . . stampeder?" asked Chris.

"Some no good low life that sneak up and scare the herd into running away. If they are lucky they get to collect a few head that we miss and then they can sell them," explained the man. He dismounted and handed the reins to a cowboy standing close by. "Get down off you're horse and let's talk a while . . . the rest of you go on about your business."

Chris climbed down from his horse and held out his hand. "Sir, my name is Chris."

"John Morgan . . . I'm the trail boss." The man grasped his hand and they shook. He was over six foot tall, in his late forties, with jet black hair which he wore long, almost to his shoulders. He was in need of a bath and a shave quite a few days in the past. He wore bat wing chaps as did all the men on horse back. John's chaps were covered with speckled brown and white hair and a large M was branded on each leg at the bottom.

"Chris . . . is that all . . . or is there more?"

Chris looked around to see who else could hear. "No, Sir . . . Christopher Le Monte," he said softly.

"Where you from . . . Chris?"

"Near Baton Rouge, sir."

"Are you a Cajun?"

"Yes, Sir."

"So this is the first time you ever saw a cattle drive."

"Yes, Sir . . . why did they laugh?"

"Chris . . . there're no cows in the whole bunch," he said with a smile "you see they are all 'Steers."

"Steers?" Chris had a puzzled look on his face.

"A steer is a male that has been castrated." The man's face was all smiles. "When's the last time you ate a good meal?"

"It's been awhile, sir," replied Chris.

"Join us for some real good grub. Old Cookie is one of the best there is when it comes to serving up some chuck wagon chow."

An elderly man in his late sixties with very little hair left on his head said to Chris as they waited in line to get their food. "There is one thing about Cookies fix-en-s . . . he'll serve you horse meat and beans anytime of the day, or night. The only trouble is . . . he never unharness 'em before he cooks 'em." Everyone laughed a little.

"Masters . . . you keep that up and I'll cook your boots," yelled Cookie.

Chris's tin plate was filled with meat and beans by Cookie, then he placed two chunks of bread on top. "Help your self to the coffee," he said. "The next joker who makes wise cracks about my cookin' will find his butt in the river." Again they all laughed.

Chris found a seat on a log nearby and ate his food in quiet. The others kept joking and talking about the events of the day. John Morgan placed his empty plate into a tub filled with dishwater. He refilled his cup with coffee and then gave one of the cowboys his order for riding 'night hawk.' Then he came to set down near Chris.

"Chris you want to join our little cattle drive?"

"Well sir, I could use a job," replied Chris.

"It'll take us about another six weeks to reach Abilene Kansas . . . the pay is a dollar a day and two meals a day."

"Six weeks . . . that's forty two days," said Chris "for a total of forty two dollars."

"I pay a bonus at the end of the drive," said John "You stay with us all the way and you get double pay."

"Forty two days . . . that's . . . eighty four dollars."

"And you get to keep one of the horses from your string."

"I got a horse already."

"If you sign on . . . I buy your horse . . . I'll give you ten dollars for him. That way if something happens to him on the trail then you're not out any loss."

"My mount is worth more than ten dollars."

"Has he been trained to work cattle?"

"No . . . but"

"Ten dollars . . . and at the end of the trail you can have him back, or any one you want."

"Eighty Four and ten . . . that comes to ninety four dollars . . . for forty two days work."

"Don't forget to tell him about all the free dirt he can eat," said a tall and very thin cowboy walking over.

"Chris this bean pole is Sam Wakefield . . . our 'Ram Rod.' He's second in command here . . . any time you need something and I'm not around . . . you go to him."

Sam held out his hand and they shook. "Any experience with cattle?" asked Sam.

"No . . . he's just a green horn . . . better put him with Drago and Pinto on drag."

"Okay," said Sam "like I said all the free dirt you can eat."

"You forgot one thing," said Chris.

"What's that?" asked John.

"What if I decide not to join up?"

"In that case . . . you can sleep here tonight . . . have breakfast with us in the morning . . . then be on your way . . . however we don't ever want to see your face around us again," said John harshly "Is that clear?"

"How close to Kansas City is this . . . where did you say you were headed?"

"Abilene . . . . Kansas City is about a hundred and fifty miles . . . I guess, maybe more," said Sam. "Is that where you're headed?"

"Yes sir," said Chris "more, or less . . . so when do I get the ten dollars for my horse?"

"Right now," said John Morgan pulling out his wallet and holding out two five dollar bills "let me warn you of one thing . . . I own all the live stock on this drive. You decide to quit . . . you're afoot . . . if you try to leave with one of my horses . . . I'll hang you for a horse thief. So if you decide to quit . . . make sure it's close to a town. You can draw your pay and leave any time you want."

"Why so hard?" asked Chris.

"Son, it's a hard world we live in . . . good cowboys are very hard to find . . . warm bodies like yourself are dime a dozen . . . and then . . . well, good horses are rare indeed. Don't worry about it . . . you'll be treated fairly . . . just do your work and we'll get along just fine."

Chris took the money.

"One more thing" explained John "if we lose the herd, there will be no pay. Every thing I have is wrapped up in those steers. You still want to join us?

"I believe I do . . . better than starving, or getting lost."

"He'll need a string of horses," said Sam.

"Give him 'Widow's Rights' to Lester's string and gear," said John.

"Widow's rights," asked Chris.

"Lester . . . he was killed in a river crossing last week," said Sam "You can have his string of six horses and his working gear . . . saddle, chaps, bull whip, ropes, bedroll and any thing else . . . they're all kept in the Chuck Wagon."

"One last thing . . . you leave that pistol with Cookie," said John "The cattle spook too easily as it is . . . so there'll be no shooting around the herd."

"Where do I bunk for the night?" asked Chris.

"Any where you want . . . under the stars," said John pointing up, and then he turned to walk away.

"Carlos will take you with him in the morning and get you squared away. For the next few days you stay real close to him," said Sam and then he too walked away to bed down for the night.

"Yes, sir," said Chris and he threw a sloppy two finger salute after them. He rose from his seat and took his empty dishes to the chuck wagon. "Where do these go?" he asked Cookie.

"Set 'em on the tail gate there, or give 'em to 'Little Mary' over there," he said pointing to one place and then to another.

"Little Mary?" Chris said looking puzzled at the young boy washing dishes in a large tub of dishwater.

"Frankie," said Cookie "he's my helper . . . so he's called 'Little Mary."

"Okay . . . if you say so . . . now where can I find Lester's things?"

"You claiming widow's rights?" asked Cookie.

"Yes . . . that's what Sam said."

"So, old John's got himself another fool . . . does he? They're in the chuck wagon in that large tote sack and the saddle is on the side there," said Cookie.

"We're going the same way," said Chris "besides I can always use the money."

"The money . . . humph . . . what money . . . just might be adding your stuff to that sack too . . . afore we's ta hit Abilene," said Cookie as he pointed to the sack under the wagon seat. "Take my advice . . . and hit the road on your own, boy."

"The name is Chris," he insisted.

"Excuse me . . . Mister Chris," roared Cookie. "Oh yeah . . . better leave that 'pop gun' with me."

Chris unbuckled the gun belt and swung the weapon over to Cookie. "Take good care of it . . . it was a gift from a friend."

"He'd a done you better if he'd gave you a swift kick in the pants for even wanting a thing like this," Cookie rolled the belt around the holster and gun then placed it into a large box in the wagon. The box was full of pistols and rifles. "Take your plunder away from here so's I can get on with my chores. Any extras you got, I keep in the wagon for ya."

All the cowboys were bedded down near the fire. Chris took the sack of gear and went quietly some distance from the camp and tried the items on, one at a time. He found a black shirt and pants fit him to a 'T.' The former owner had very large feet, so the boots were too big. He pulled out a long leather braded whip. He tossed one end out on the ground.

"You know how to use that thing?" the voice came from behind him. The man setting in the saddle was a Mexican. "My name's Carlos," he said "you must be Chris."

"That's right . . . as for this . . . I never saw one this long before."

"We use them to keep the steers moving," said Carlos as he walked his horse up to Chris and dismounted. "In the hands of a skilled vaquero he can make a steer climb a tree."

"That I'd like to see," Chris held out his hand to Carlos as he came near but the Mexican ignored it.

"Sam said I was to teach you to be a vaquero."

"Vaquero . . . what's that?"

"Spanish for cowboy," said Carlos. "You'll need this . . . and this . . . not this . . . or this" he said as he picked through the items. "Put all the rest in the sack and give it to Cookie."

"Okay . . . Carlos . . . what's next?"

"Bed down and I'll get you up in the morning . . . that's when school really starts." He quickly remounted and rode away.

§

Chris found out that being a cowboy was not all fun and games, least wise not riding drag on a cattle drive. The trail drive was heading north, more or less, so anytime the wind was blowing, in any direction, other than south, the dust would drift away from him. However when the wind happened to travel in a southerly direction, he would choke on the dust. It would fill his eyes, nose and throat. At times like this he was sure sorry he had signed on as a 'Drover.' Carlos, Drago and Pinto taught him a few things about being a cowboy as the days rolled by. Carlos was in charge of the remuda. He taught Chris how to recognize his string of horses, all six of them. They each had more cattle savvy then he did at first, but he soon caught on to the ways of a steer and how to persuade the critter to keep up with the herd.

Cookie would always serve good food and lots of it. Frankie, 'Little Mary' would scamper around the Chuck Wagon doing what ever needed to be done for Cookie. One evening Frankie made a bad mistake when he happened to spill a cup of hot coffee on one of the cowboys. The unfortunate one was a nasty sort of ruffian by the name of Bruce. If he had a last name no one could recall it.

Bruce took great offence at being bathed with the hot coffee. He took out after Frankie while the others all laughed. Frankie was terrified of the large man chasing him so he ran away from camp. About fifty yards away Bruce caught him. He took the little fellow down and began to beat him with his fists as Frankie screamed for help.

The scene of his mother being beaten to death flashed though Chris's mind, he jumped to his feet and ran toward them as did the others. They all gathered around as Bruce kept hitting Frankie. Chris picked up a large piece of dead wood and hit Bruce across the back as hard as he could. Bruce screamed with the pain and fell to one side. Chris then helped Frankie to his feet. The little boy was bleeding badly about the mouth and eyes.

"Take him to the Chuck Wagon," ordered Chris as he past him to a couple of the other cowboys.

"You son-of-a-bitch," screamed Bruce as he rose from the ground "I'm gonna kill you."

"The little fellow's had enough," said Chris "you're about to kill him."

"Now, I'm going to kill you," said Bruce as he flexed his back muscles. He drew a large knife from one of his boots. "Say your prayers." He moved closer to Chris.

Looking around Chris could see the others were only going to watch, not one of them was going to help, or try to stop it. He backed away as the big man kept coming closer. Chris was backed nearly to the camp when John Morgan rode up.

"What the Hell is going on here?" he demanded "Bruce, put away that knife."

"That brat poured some hot coffee on me and this knot head hit me with a chunk of wood," yelled Bruce "so I'm ah fixin' to do me some carving on his face."

"I said to put that knife away," demanded John very loudly.

Bruce hesitated for a few moments. There was the crack of a whip and the knife went flying from Bruce's hand. He held his hand as the pain reached his brain. Carlos was standing a few feet away with a bull whip unrolled; he began to roll it up once more.

"Jefe said to put the knife away."

John went to the chuck wagon. Cookie had Frankie lying on a blanket beside the wagon. He was trying to stop the bleeding.

"How's he doing?" asked John.

"He's hurt real bad," sniffed Cookie as he fought the tears back.

"Do the best you can for him," said John as he patted the man on the back.

"It ain't gonna be enough," and he broke out in tears.

"Bruce damn you . . . if this lad dies and I'll hang you from the nearest tree," yelled John.

"He poured hot coffee on me," yelled Bruce "and this one clubbed me from behind."

"Still that's no reason to beat the lad," yelled John "tie him to the wagon . . . I wanna make sure you're still here in the morning." Six cowboys tackled him and bound him hand and foot. John turned to face Chris "what were you thinking of . . . stepping in like that?"

"Frankie . . . he was out classed . . . no one else would help him."
"Nobody ever wants to face Bruce," said John "he's just plain mean."

"I'm glad you came along when you did."

"Are you now?" asked John "What are you going to do when I'm not around to stop him the next time?" He turned and walked back to the Chuck Wagon.

A rider came hard and fast into the camp. He pulled up and was on the ground before the horse stopped his forward motion. "Mister Morgan," shouted the rider. It was Bob, the scout and the same cowboy who caught Chris as he watched the herd. "We've got real trouble coming this way and in a damn big hurry," He said all excited.

"What sort of trouble?" asked John as he came to meet with Bob. Every one of the cowboys came running to hear what the trouble was.

"Prairie fire," shouted Bob.

"Where and how far?" demanded John.

"Southwest of here . . . at the rate it's moving . . . maybe two hours . . . maybe a lot less."

"What're we gonna do?" shouted the cowboys together.

"The river . . . ah . . . the Cimarron, it's just ahead . . . how much water is there?" asked John.

"Its low this time of year," said Bob "but that just might do . . . we might save most of the herd . . . if we can get them across in time."

"Everybody . . . get your guns and mount up . . . we'll stampede the herd . . . . Maybe we can out run the fire to the river," shouted John. In a very short span of time all the cowboys were mounted on their horses and gathered behind the cattle. John fired his pistol into the air and the cattle began to run away from the report of the weapon. Then some of the other cowboys began to fire their guns to further frighten the herd.

Chris felt dressed now that his revolver was once more at his side and he too fired his gun into the air. The cattle were running all out at a break neck pace through the darkness. There was a light overcast of clouds in the night sky. Soon the air was filled with the sent of burning grass, weeds, wood and anything else caught in the path of the fire. Chris's mount became nervous as his nostrils began to get a whiff of the smoke and he became more frightened then the cattle racing along beside him. The stronger the smoke became the more the horse panicked.

The night air was filled with choking dust from the livestock and the smoke from the fire. It became more and more difficult to see anything in the darkness. Chris felt something hit him in the face. He let go of the reins and nearly fell from the saddle. He was knocked backwards and he grabbed for the saddle horn to stay seated. Then something else hit him in the face, this time he was knocked clear of his mount, which kept running as fast as it could. All around him he could hear the sounds of animals running. He staggered to his feet and bumped into a large tree. The limb that knocked him off his horse was within easy reach, so he quickly climbed up into the tree. He had just reached safety on the tree branch when part of the herd came rushing though below him. He would have been trampled to death if he had remained on the ground. He stayed in the tree as more cattle ran past.

Chris looked to the southwest and to his horror he could now see the light of the flames in the distance. He waited until all the livestock had passed, and then he dropped to the ground. There was no where to escape the oncoming fire so he started to run after the herd. He drew his sixgun and fired three quick shots. It was a signal for help the cowboys had told him about. Then he continued to run. A few minutes later he fired thee more shots and ran some more. Soon it began to get lighter as the fire closed in on him. He fired three shots again as he ran. The smoke was very thick and hot as it gained on him. He was having trouble breathing as the dense cloud of hot gases swirled around him.

He suddenly fell into a deep raven and landed face down into some water. In the fire light he could see the ditch was wide and barren of anything that would burn. The water was muddy and stagnant, but it could protect him from the heat of the fire. He quickly covered his body with the brackish goop. He placed his handkerchief in the waters then tied it over his whole head. He filled his hat with water and placed it tightly on top of his head. He pulled his shirt up to his eyebrows and breathed through the wet clothes to help cut the thick smoke. As the flames passed over him he kept throwing water over his body. Despite the cooling effect of the water it was sill like taking a very hot bath.

When at last the fire subsided around him, he washed the mud from his body, then his gun as best he could and then pulled himself out of the waters. He removed his boots which were water logged, to dry them out. He was exhausted from the night's activities, so he curled up on the dry ground to rest, and soon he fell asleep.

§

"How many did we lose?" asked John. Sam and Bob rode up to where John was setting in the shade of a big cotton wood tree the next morning. They were on the north side of the river. The cowboys were gathering up the cattle which were scattered all over.

"Not more than five hundred," said Sam.

"That's not too bad . . . five hundred out of five thousand," said John "how about the horses?"

"It'll take a day, or more to round them all up," said Carlos as he rode up to join the trio.

"How many horses we got?" asked John.

"About two horses to a man . . . that's all we got right now," said Carlos.

"Alright . . . we camp here for two days . . . round up what we can . . . then we push on to Abilene," commanded John. "Anybody, seen the chuck wagon?"

"Not since the crossing last night," said Sam.

"You get the livestock rounded up and I'll look for the chuck wagon," said John. They spurred their mounts to ride away in different directions. John began the long ride back to the river crossing some few miles back. He repeated his plan to any cowboy he came across. About noon time he found the chuck wagon stuck in the mud on the north side of the river. It was buried in tight. He rode up to it and asked "How's Frankie doing?"

"He's sleeping right now," said Cookie. "Poor kid had a real bad time last night."

"Now we got to get you out of there," he threw his rope around the tongue of the wagon and then wrapped the other end around his saddle horn. With his horse and the team pulling together on the wagon, it still would not budge. "You wait and I'll go get some of the men to help get you out of there."

"I'll be right here," said Cookie.

65

John rode south across the river and up onto a hill. He could see for miles from this vantage point. North of the river he could see several cowboys herding some cattle into a larger group, others were driving some northward. He watched for anyone near the river for a few minutes. When some time past, he turned his gaze to the south once more and shook his head at the burned out sight before him. He pulled at the reins to once again ride north, when something caught his eye. He turned the horse again toward the south and to a halt. He watched very carefully for a few seconds.

"I thought I saw something," he said out loud to himself. A few more seconds past "I guess not." He wheeled his mount around and rode back across the river.

§

The suns rays reached down into the gully and warmed the sleeping young man. He soon began to stir as the rays became hotter. Chris stretched his limbs and stood to his feet. He reached down and retrieved his boots; they were still damp from being in the pool of water, but he pulled them on anyway. He stood looking at the water he had taken a mud bath in during the fire, although there was an aching in his throat for a drink, he just shook his head and moved toward a trail leading up to level ground. When he climbed out of the ditch he could hardly believe his eyes. Every thing was black as far as he was able to see, there was nothing that was not burnt black. A few head of dead cattle lay scattered about on the ground, they too were burned black.

Chris started to walk northward. He kept his eyes on the horizon hoping to see one of the cowboys. Maybe they would ride back to see if he was still alive. He pushed on though the day and into the night time. His thirst was beginning to make him wish he had filled up in that mud hole. Now there was no sign of anything green to indicate where water could be found. There was a lot less heat in the night air, and he felt cold. To build a fire, he would need some thing to burn, however the fire had burned all of it. He kept moving all through the night. The thirst became unbearable as the morning sun peaked over the eastern skyline. He fell down on the ground among some large rocks. He dragged himself into a setting position so he could see toward the north once more.

Chris heard a buzzing noise off to his left. He turned his head in the direction of the noise to see a coiled rattle snake about six feet from him. He searched the area over carefully, taking note of the rocks. His hand was like lightning and the revolver spit fire and lead. The rattler's head went flying to one side. Chris quickly grabbed the snake's body. He stripped off the hide and then began to devour the flesh of the reptile. The juices of the snake wetted his thirst and the flesh satisfied his hunger. When the snake was devoid of any flesh, he fell back into the scant shade of the rocks to sleep for a while.

§

John Morgan spent a restless night in camp on the north side of the river. All of the cowboys had been accounted for except for Chris and Bruce. No one had seen either of them since they stampeded the cattle. Early that morning John rode back across the river and upon a hill he waited for several minutes. Then he saw something in the distance.

"I was right," he said to himself "I did see something yesterday." He spurred his horse into action to ride hard to the south across the charred remains of the prairie. As he got closer he could make out the sure signs of it being a man on foot. He soon rode up as Chris staggered along. When John rode up to him, Chris fell to the ground. John quickly gave him a drink from his canteen. "Easy does it."

§

"You ate what?" asked one of the cowboys.

"A rattle snake," said Chris. He was recounting his experience in the camp that night to those present.

"Raw?" said the cowboy with a disgusted expression on his face.

"The fire burned everything . . . and I needed the juices to keep me from dying of thirst."

"I heard you Cajuns would eat anything . . . but this sure beats all I ever heard of before," said another cowboy.

"There's no way I'm gonna eat a rattle snake . . . cooked, or raw," gagged another.

"You'd be surprised at what you'd eat just to stay alive," said John. "A human will do most anything to keep on living."

"Did you ever eat a shake?" asked one of the cowboys.

"Can't say that I have . . . but I believe . . . given the same set of circumstances, I sure could . . . and probably ask for seconds." They all laughed.

§

Abilene was a small town built on both sides of the railroad tracks which divided it into two different towns. South of the tracks was the 'Shady Side' and to the north of the tracks was the 'Respectable Side' where the upper crust of town folks lived and did business. The cowboys hit the saloons and other places of rest and relaxation full tilt. Their guns were blazing as horses galloped up and down the street. Just after dark it became a little less noisy as they managed to become more intoxicated.

Chris spent some time at the barber shop where he got a hair cut then took a long hot bath. He then went to the General Store north of the tracks and purchased a new suit of clothes. Black jacket and pants, a white shirt with laced front, a hat and new boots also black. He trimmed it with a thin black ribbon tie. His old clothing and weapon he placed into a tote sack. He then went to the railroad station and asked the station master "When's the next train to Kansas City?"

"Tomorrow morning . . . at ten twenty," said the little man seated at a desk with the key to the telegraph at his elbow. "You want a ticket?"

"How much?"

"Ten dollars," was the reply.

"Ten days hard work," Chris mused. He turned to leave.

"You want a ticket or not?"

"I'll let you know in the morning," he said as he walked out the door. All the street lamps had been lit and the sun was no longer in sight. The last of the red clouds in the west could be seen. He strolled along the board walk for a few yards. He was stopped by four men,

68

each carrying shotguns, plus one tall long haired man in a long black duster. He had two pistols stuffed into his red sash, butt ends forward.

"You one of them drovers that just came in today?" asked the long haired man standing in the middle.

"That's right," said Chris.

"You were told to keep south of the 'Dead Line," said the man loudly.

"What I wanted was north of the rails," said Chris.

"There are no loose women on this side of the tracks," said the man.

"No . . . you see I wanted some new cloths and a good nights rest in the hotel, then tomorrow I'm going to take the train to Kansas City."

"Is that a fact," said the man "your kind belongs in the hotel south of the tracks, so get moving." He pointed the way with his thumb.

"Why so unfriendly?" asked Chris.

"We let one of your kinds up here . . . . The next thing we know you'll all be up here."

"As you wish," said Chris taking steps in the direction indicated by the brace of shotguns. They walked twenty feet behind him to the rails, there they stopped and stood watching as he went toward the hotel on the south side of the tracks.

He crossed the street running parallel to the rails and stood on the boardwalk in front of the hotel. He looked up and down the street. All the horses were in the large corral at the stock yards, but all the cowboys were inside the saloons. Music was flowing from inside each one of the half dozen or so that lined the street. As he stood there he wondered what it would be like in Kansas City. Just then one of his fellow companions on the trail drive ran from inside one of the saloons. Out in the street he turned to fire his pistol at someone exiting from inside the bar room. The cowboy must have missed his target; however the other man did not miss. His shot dropped the unfortunate man right there. Chris quickly went to the side of the unfortunate cowboy. It was Bob the scout and he was dead from a bullet to the chest.

"Well, well ... what have we here," said the deadly marksman "I do believe it's the Cajun who likes to interfere in other peoples business."

Chris looked up into the face of Bruce. "We thought you perished in the fire."

"No such luck," said Bruce as he reloaded his pistol. "You fellows were trying so hard to save that miserable herd ... me ... I just wiggled loose and rode away."

"That figures ... you being a coward and all," said Chris rising to stand face to face with the large bully.

"That's right ... we do have some unfinished business ... don't we?" said Bruce loudly.

"Friends of yours," Chris asked looking behind Bruce to see the stern faces of two men standing close.

"You might say that," said Bruce.

"So that's where you get your courage," said Chris in a nasty tone.

"You packing a gun?" asked Bruce "Cause I'm a fixin' to settle our differences once and for all ways."

"It's in the bag," said Chris as he held it up waist high.

"Put it on," said Bruce "Don't want it said you didn't have a fair chance." He chuckled and the other two joined in.

Chris looked around at those watching. No one was going to help him in any way. All of them were just going to watch as someone else was going to be killed. The death of Bob was not enough for them for now they were hungry for more blood shed. He opened the bag and slowly removed the gun belt, holster and sixgun. He then dropped the bag to the ground and commenced to place the leather laden with the weapon around his waist. He removed his jacket and let it fall to the ground. He then stretched his arms out wide then lowered them to his sides. His right hand he placed a few inches away from the butt of the gun.

"He looks real dangerous," said Bruce in a loud and mocking voice.

"You better watch out," said one of his cohorts "he might actually get that pea shooter out of the holster."

"You better forget it," said Chris sternly "I can kill you."

"Is that a fact," said Bruce in the same mocking voice. "Say your prayers kid 'cause I'm gonna blow a hole clean through you."

Chris watched his face and the other two standing a few feet to either side of Bruce. His smile slowly disappeared as the man poised his hand to draw his weapon. His eyes narrowed and his mouth tightened. He started his draw. Chris's bullet hit him in the chest. Bruce's gun was not quite out of the holster when he pulled the trigger and the weapon fired through the holster and into the ground beside his right foot. For a split second no one moved. The other two could not believe that Bruce had been beaten and was hit. When he fell forward onto the ground, they each started to draw their weapons to avenge the death of their friend. Twice more Chris fired his pistol. They both were hit before they could fire a shot at him. The one to the right, clutched at his torso as he turned where he stood and fell forward to the ground. The other one paused for a moment. He was holding his chest with one hand while his other was holding his drawn gun. He looked at Chris then slowly raised it to point in his direction. Chris fired once more and the man dropped to his knees where he pulled the trigger sending the shot into the ground a few feet in front of him. Then he fell, face down in the dirt.

Chris quickly reloaded his revolver and returned it to the holster. He then picked up his jacket and shook off the dirt then placed it over his arm. He retrieved the bag containing his old clothing. A couple of the cowboys came to his side wanting to shake his hand and congratulate him. Other people gathered around the four dead men lying in the street. Some of them took cloths and dipped it into the fresh blood of the men. Others began to take items off their bodies.

"Leave them alone," shouted Chris "What are you . . . people . . . or vultures?" Everyone moved back several feet but remained in a wide semi-circle round about the dead men. "Some one . . . get them off the street," yelled Chris.

"That my job," said a fellow hurrying up the street. He was followed by two younger men pushing a cart along. From their dress it was apparent they were Chinese "I undertaker for Abilene." They stopped the two wheeled cart next to the four men on the ground. Then they picked up the body of Bob and placed it onto the cart. They returned to pick up another, but Chris spoke.

"Leave them there," said Chris "They don't deserve to ride with Bob."

"We must clean street," said the elder Chinaman "it is job we do for Abilene."

"You can come back later to get the others," said Chris. "This one was a friend so you do him right."

"It will be done, as you wish," said the Chinaman and the three bowed.

"What the hell is going on here?" demanded a man running toward the scene. He stopped a few feet from the three left on the ground. On his chest was a small tin star in a circle, it carried the letters that spelled out the words of "Town Marshal."

"That one in the center shot that one on the cart there," said a cowboy stepping forward. "Then the three of them tried to shoot him" he was pointing at Chris "but he managed to get all three of them first."

"Is that right?" asked the Town Marshal coming to face Chris. He didn't say a word only nodded his head. He kept his gaze at the man's face as he shifted the bag of clothing to his left hand. Then he placed his right hand near his pistol.

"He didn't want to fight, but they goaded him into it," said another cowboy.

"That the way it happened?" asked the Marshal staring deep into Chris eyes.

"That's the way of it," replied Chris with a sigh.

"Hand over the gun," demanded the Marshal. Chris hesitated for a moment then complied by slowly removing the gun from the holster and handed it butt first to him. "Aren't you a little bit young to be a gunfighter, just how old are you?"

"Sixteen," replied Chris.

"Well . . . youngster, it looks like you're on your way to an early grave," said the Marshal "I can't hold you for this . . . cause it looks like a clear case of 'self defense' to me. However, what I am going to do is to run you out of town before some other fool decide he's faster then you. So go get your self killed some where else, but stay out of my town."

"I'll need my horse," said Chris.

"I'll walk you to the corral and see to it that you leave town right now."

Chris walked to the corral where his horse was with all the others. He saddled the animal as the Marshal watched. He opened the gate and led the horse outside then closed it.

"Chris," called John Morgan to him as he was about to mount his horse "wait a minute."

Chris turned to face his old boss man as he came hurrying along the street.

"He's leaving town right now," said the town Marshal loudly.

"Give me a minute, or two with him," said John very sternly as he drew near to them. "It's the middle of the night . . . for goodness shakes."

"I don't care . . . the sooner he's gone the sooner I can get my sleep."

"Hold your horses," shouted John "Chris, where're you going?"

"You know where," he replied nodding his head toward the Marshal.

"No, no Chris," pleaded John "what happened here tonight will be all over the country come morning. If you go . . . there . . . they'll be waiting for you. This lawman will only run you out of his town, but the lawmen there will just shoot you on sight."

"Where else can I go?"

"Marshal, will you excuse us?" The lawman looked at each of them in turn then slowly walked about twenty feet away where he leaned against the corral fence with one hand. Then John said quietly "Come with me . . . to my ranch in Texas. There you can hide out for a couple of years till this whole thing blows over . . . by then everyone will have forgotten all about it.

"You want a real cowboy, or do you just want the reward on my head?"

"If I just wanted the reward . . . all I'd have to do is tell that lawman who you are," said John. "You come with me to Texas . . . there you'll be safe for a while. Besides I need a good cowboy . . . you know how few and far between they are."

"I'm just a green horn."

"You may be . . . but you'll make one fine vaquero in a couple of years," said John holding out his hand. "What do you say?" Chris saw the smile on John's face, the sincerity in his eyes, and he remembered the man had always treated him fairly all the time they were together.

"You got a green horn." They shook hands.

"Times up . . . he's leaving right now," said the Marshal.

"He's on his way . . . the chuck wagon is about a mile out in that direction," he pointed and Chris mounted his horse "I'll see you in the morning," said John.

"My gun," said Chris as he stopped his horse close to the Marshal.

The lawman handed the gun to him. "Its empty." he held out the rounds in his other hand. "If you'll take my advice . . . throw this thing into the river and leave all guns alone."

"Marshal, you may not believe me, but I really wish I could, so long."

§

"Where the hell is the little bastard?" screamed Phillip "it's been almost a year since he ran away."

"That Indian . . . what's his name?" cried Bernie.

"Cherokee Tom . . . no . . . ah . . . oh hell . . . Seminole," stammered Phillip. He went to the desk in the study of their home and dug though some papers. "Choctaw Charlie," he said, as he read the letter they had received from him.

"Choctaw Charlie says he went to Texas," said Bernie.

"I know that . . . but where?" screamed Phillip.

"Phil, Texas is a big place . . . there's lots of places he could be hiding," said Bernie.

"Why the hell, don't you tell me something I don't already know?" pleaded Phillip in a loud voice "and stop calling me Phil."

"Choctaw Charlie says he'll find him sooner, or later, but he wants more money to do so."

"How much?" asked Phillip.

"Two Thousand," said Bernie.

"Okay . . . promise him two thousand . . . any thing . . . only find him."

"Are you serious?" whined Bernie.

"What we promise to pay this . . . half breed and what he gets . . . is two different things," said Phillip. "When we find him . . . we'll just burry two bodies instead of one." A smile came over his lips and then they both laughed out loud.

§

"You call this country home?" asked Chris as he rode along side the chuck wagon.

"Yep," said Cookie "my piece of the pie was my grandfather's . . . he took it away from a bunch of Mexicans. That was back in forty nine. They were against the union troops. Then it past to my father, that was back in sixty three. Grandpa went to war for the Confederates. We

75

never saw hide or hair of him ever again. Then it past to me, that was in seventy two when a Comanche riding party put an arrow in pa's back."

"You actually raise cattle out here?" asked Chris.

"Why not . . . its cattle country isn't it?"

"What do they eat? I mean there's nothing in the way of grass." Chris asked, as he looked out at the barren county side of West Texas.

"Young feller, don't be so dad blame right all the time." Cookie whipped up the horses and increased their speed for a few yards. They soon slowed back down to a gentle pace once more.

"John, I was wondering . . ." Chris started but John cut him off.

"Well don't," he said and spurred his mount to ride on ahead.

Chris turned to look at the other cowboys riding with them. They were all smiles at his dilemma about the dry country they were riding through. There was nothing, but grease wood and scrubby mesquite trees as far as the eye could see. Sprinkled here and there were a few prickly pear cacti. All the creek beds were dry. Not a sign of water or anything really green had he seen since they crossed that last river called the Canadian. The further south they rode the dryer it became. It had been like this for several days as they rode though this country.

§

Late one morning they came to a group of little shacks setting on a rise in the terrain. They were close together and stood some distance apart from a larger building. They were all weather beaten and each one was sorely in need of repair some time in the ancient past. The larger building had some horses tied to the hitching rails out in front.

As they approached, all the cowboys began to holler "A saloon . . . boy, am I ever thirsty . . . let's get a drink," and then they sped forwards. Chris held back as the others raced to the building. He looked the place over really well as he inched his way to the building. John Morgan also held back from rushing into the old building. He tied his horse to the hitching post. Cookie parked the wagon, with the brake on, out in the road in front of the saloon. Then he too raced into the building. Frankie sat on the seat of the wagon and watched them as the others scampered inside. Chris was the last to enter the building.

He took his time to pause at the door way and read the room several times before he entered.

Four men were seated at a table, they were playing cards. Two more were standing at the far end of the bar, which was nothing more than a couple of planks nailed together placed on a pair of old beer kegs. One man was seated at a table in one corner of the room. Then there was the bartender. He was busy setting glasses on the bar and pouring drinks for the cowboys which had just entered the place. John went to a table just inside the door and seated himself. He placed his hat on the table and wiped the sweat from his face as he waited to be served. Chris entered slowly and crossed the floor to stand at the near end of the bar. There he waited to receive his turn at the liquid refreshments. One of the men in the card game yelled out "ya'll want a join in for a few hands?"

"No thanks," was the general reply from the three cowboys and Cookie at the bar.

"How about you mister?" he asked of John.

"I don't play cards," was John's reply.

The four men at the table spoke quietly among themselves for a few seconds then they rose and walked up behind those at the bar and stood spread out in a line a foot or two apart.

"You hombres returning from a cattle drive?" asked the tall man in the line.

"That's right," said Cookie.

"Well then . . . you must have lots of cash on you."

"I hate to disappoint you mister," said John "Wells Fargo has all our money . . . all we got is just some pocket money for minor expenses."

"Well now . . . sees as how you won't play cards with us . . . I guess we'll just have to take it from you. Maybe even your horses and gear too."

"Look mister . . . we don't want any trouble," said John. Chris removed the strap on his side arm and stepped around the end of the bar and stood poised to draw if the occasion called for it. "We just want a few cold drinks then we'll be on our way."

"You don't understand . . . we aim to strip you fellows clean of everything you got."

"Don't touch those guns . . . or I'll kill you," said Chris.

"Who the hell are you, kid?" the braggart snickered.

"Nobody . . . we just want to be left alone," said Chris. "Now you don't want to die, and I don't want to kill you."

"Get the little squirt," said the mouthy one as he snickered. "Mister we intend to leave you alone, but out on the range with nothing . . . now strip." They each began to draw their weapons. Chris fired rapidly and dropped three of them. The braggart was the first one to fall. The cowboys standing at the bar managed to wound the one remaining. Cookie dropped to the floor. The two men at the end of the bar joined Cookie on the floor.

"You dead?" asked one of the cowboys as he knelt beside Cookie.

"Is this Texas?" asked Cookie.

"Why . . . yeah . . . it's Texas," replied the cowboy.

"Then I aint dead." He got to his feet.

"Don't kill me," pleaded the last of the four. "I didn't want to do it . . . they made me."

"Shut up," screamed one of the cowboys. He raised his weapon to the man's head.

"Don't," said Chris "there's been too much blood spilled already." He reloaded his gun and walked out the door. Each of the cowboys grabbed a bottle or two and ran after him. They quickly mounted and rode around the building shooting and yelling. Cookie climbed aboard the chuck wagon and whipped up the horses to leave in a big hurry. John threw some money on the bar then came outside with his revolver in hand and cocked. He watched those inside for any more attempts to do harm to him, or his men. Chris walked to his horse and mounted. He pulled along side John as they rode out of the area at a slow trot.

"What makes men act like that?" he asked.

"I wish I knew," replied John "believe me Chris . . . I wish I knew."

"What is this?" screamed Phillip "you expect me to believe this nonsense . . . a shooting in Abilene Kansas, then another shooting in some hell hole in Texas . . . and you think it's Christopher Le Monte who doing the shooting?"

"I tell you it's him," pleaded Choctaw Charlie. "Bucky taught the kid to shoot."

"Hog wash," said Phillip as he paced the floor of his room in a Waco Texas hotel. "This can't possibly be the same person doing the shooting. I tell you it's two different people."

"No, no, it's him . . . the same person . . . the descriptions in both shootings match the kid."

"You say this . . . Bucky . . . person taught him to shoot. Just how good is this fellow . . . Bucky with a gun?"

"I never saw anyone better," said Charlie.

"I want to talk to this pistolero . . . maybe he knows where, or how we can find him."

"That's not possible," said Charlie softly.

"Not possible . . . why the hell not?" demanded Phillip. The Indian took his knife and drew it across his throat. "I see . . . dead men tell no tails, huh."

"Now how do we find him?" asked Bernie.

"You go with Charlie to this place in . . . where ever in west Texas and see if you can pick up his trail. It shouldn't be to hard . . . he leaves a trail of dead men where ever he's been."

"What are you going to do, Phil?" asked Bernie.

"I'm going to Washington to see someone who just might be able to help us" replied Phillip, "and stop calling me PHIL."

§

"Sheriff," said a man in a ditch out near the Weston's farm "We're draining this swamp when we came across the remains of a body." He stood pointing to a partially uncovered skeleton which appeared to be human.

"Just leave it alone until Doc can get a good look at it," he said. "Keep your men out of this area and we'll let you know when you can resume your work."

"Sheriff, you sent for me?" asked an elderly man dressed in an expensive silk suite driving up in a single horse drawn buggy.

"Yeah Doc," said the Sheriff "look's like the workmen here have uncovered us a mystery. You take over and let me know what . . . who . . . when . . . and all the other things you can." The doctor stepped down and went to the edge of the ditch.

"This may take a few days . . . from the looks of the bones . . . I would say it may take a month or more."

"Well do the best you can as fast as you can . . . will you?" said the Sheriff.

"I can only do one thing at a time," said the Doctor as he climbed down a short ladder into the ditch to begin his examination. "I'll let you know . . . if and when I know."

§

"Mister Weston," said the fancy dressed over stuffed man puffing on a fat cigar   "Welcome to Washington sir." He held out his hand and they shook. "I was hoping to have some good news for you . . . but it seems that neither the Justice Department, nor the U S Marshall's Office is interested in pursuing the matter. Even our own State Officials want no more to do with it . . . so you see you have come a long way for nothing."

"Senator . . . there has got to be a way of bringing this murderer to justice" pleaded Phillip.

"I don't see how . . . after all . . . it was ruled justifiable by a judge, so no one wants to over turn his decision. And then the lawmen in Kansas and Texas both said the shootings were in self defense. "

"How about the U S Supreme Court?" Phillip begged.

"I have spoken to a couple of the Justices . . . but they don't want to waste their time with it either."

"So now a killer is running lose," said Phillip in a disgusted tone. "He's killed my father . . . three men in Kansas . . . and three more in Texas . . . how many more does he have to kill before someone puts a stop to it?" He was shouting at the last.

"Mister Weston . . . I know it looks that way . . . but in each instance it has been ruled 'self defense.' In fact the Texas Rangers want to make him one of them . . . when he's old enough."

"What have they got in Texas for lawmen . . . morons?"

"I'm sorry Mister Weston . . . but there is nothing I can do for you."

§

"Daddy," shouted a thin teen aged girl in pig tails riding hard to meet with John and company. She jumped from her horse to the ground and threw her arms around John, when he too had dismounted. "Daddy," she squealed once more.

"Cathy darling," he said loudly "it's good to see you."

"Oh daddy, I missed you so much."

"Let me look at you," he pushed her away and she turned around for him. She was dressed in jeans, long sleeve blouse and cowboy boots. Her straw hat was lying in the road way, a few yards back toward the house.

"My, my . . . how you have grown," he said.

"It's been nearly two years since you were last here," she squealed and ran into his arms once more. "I'm seventeen now."

"How old?" he asked.

"Okay . . . I'll be seventeen in eleven months," she said with a giggle.

"That's more like it," said John. "I brought you and your mother some things; they're in the chuck wagon."

"Who's that?" she asked spotting Chris riding among the other cowboys.

"A youngster with a big load on his back," he said softly. "He's here to hide out from the world for a while."

"A runaway?"

"Now, you leave it alone . . . and him too . . . you hear?"

"Yes Daddy," she promised.

§

Chris was assigned to the area of the ranch where the horses were kept. It was maintained by Carlos. It was about six miles from the main house where the Morgan family lived. Carlos was the one who cared for the horses and worked them with the cattle, so each horse knew what to do and what not to do with the beefs. He kept the brood mares close when it was their time to deliver. The area was by a small stream of water, with lots of grass for a few miles along its banks. There was an adobe four room house, small but adequate. It had a kitchen/dinning room, with a bedroom on either side, which was flanked by another large room that served as storage and living room. Two sets of bunk beds were in each of the two bedrooms. Just incase more cowboys came to do some work in the area. Once a month, the main house would send out supplies to feed the hands.

Chris found working the horses and caring for them was great fun at times, but it too, was work and very hard work at times. There were fences to mend, hay to stack into the make-sift barn for feed for the horses in the corrals during the hard winters. He would collapse all most asleep each night before his head could hit the pillow on his bunk.

The first day at the remuda area the windmill quit spinning. And for the next two days Chris and Carlos had to carry water for the mares in the corral about to deliver. They led the other horses out to water them in the streams. Every few days they would ride along the creek to check on the other horses. In the winter they would have to corral them and fork over lots of hay for feed.

Chris had been at the remuda for three months when during the night the mares in the delivery corral began to scream and bang against the fence and barn. Carlos was up and out the door in his long johns and boots. He placed his hat on his head as he crossed the threshold of the door. He was carrying his rifle in one hand.

Chris managed to get his pants on before the boots, he grabbed his hat and gun belt before he ran out into the cold air of the night. Carlos fired two shots at some thing in the night as it ran away in a big hurry.

Carlos went to the fence and gathered up a lantern hanging on the fence next to the gate.

"Condenar" he shouted. He turned to see Chris with his revolver in his hand. "You got fuego?"

"What?" Chris asked.

"Fire . . . match . . . to light the lanterna."

"No" replied Chris. He turned and ran back into the shack. He retrieved the box of matches from the center of the dinning table, and then returned to Carlos. They quickly lit the light and then entered the corral of mares. One was lying on the ground as the blood spilled from her neck and back. Carlos let out a long line of Spanish obscenities as he examined the mare.

"Condenar mountain lion," yelled Carlos. "She has killed one of the finest horses that Jefe owns.

"Did you hit the cat? Chris asked.

"I think so . . . maybe . . . I don't know."

"She's not dead." Chris pointed to the mare.

"She might as well be," Carlos very sadly said. "She is going to bleed to death before sunrise."

"Can't we do some thing for her?"

"Not even a doctor could stop that much bleeding and she may have more wounds on the other side."

"She's trying to get up," Chris said.

"No, she's is going to deliver," said Carlos sadly. He handed the lantern to Chris and then raised the rife to his shoulder.

"Don't shoot her," pleaded Chris "maybe we can save the colt."

"It would not live with out its mama to nurse it."

"There is one mare here that's nursing two colts," pleaded Chris "so let's try to save the colt."

"Those are gemelo . . . twins," said Carlos "well, you do what you want, Amigo. Me, I want some breakfast and get dressed . . . its cold out here."

§

Cathy heard John say the monthly supplies needed to be taken out to the remuda area, for Carlos and Chris might be down to 'licking the cans.' The supplies were over due about a week ago. He was very busy and he was not able to get loose to deliver them to the men. Betty was involved with some canning in Willow Bend, with her friend Jane.

"Daddy, I can take the supplies out to Chris."

"Chris," he quipped "I told you to keep away from him."

"Maybe they can survive on air and 'licking the cans,'" She replied sternly. "Is that what you would like for supper . . . cans to lick?"

"Oh, hell girl," John said as he came into the kitchen. "Alright you can take the supplies out to Carlos, but you stay away from Chris, you hear me."

"Yes daddy, dear."

§

She drove the buckboard up to the adobe house and then stepped down to enter the dwelling. She called out "Carlos," and then with no answer she called out with "Chris." After a few tries and no response she went to the corrals and barn.

"Hello," she called loudly "Any one here?"

"Hello, your self," called Chris as he appeared on the platform of the windmill. She stepped over to the tower. Chris came to a setting position on the frame work just below the fan blades.

"What are you doing up there?" she asked.

"Well . . . I was going to jump," he chuckled "But then I thought I might like to try flying instead of walking for a change."

"You can't fly . . . silly."

"Now you spoiled it."

"How's that?"

"Well . . . last night my fairy god mother told me I could fly . . . that is, if I believed I could, but now you have spoiled my train of thought."

"None sense," she snapped "I brought your supplies, so be so kind as to help me unload them."

"Yes ma'am," he replied and climbed down to the level ground.

"What were you doing up there anyway?" She asked.

"That old fan needed to be greased, because it's difficult to get any sleep around here, between it's squeaking and Carlos' snoring."

About that time Carlos rode into the area. When he saw them to-gether, he made a bee line to the buckboard where he dismounted at the rear of the wagon.

"Get the supplies unloaded and then get the water in the tank so the mares can have some water." Chris did as he was told. "Senorita Cathy, does your father know you are out here?"

"Yes, he does," she squirmed "he was too busy and I was the only one left to bring the supplies."

"Gracias Nina, now, if you hurry you can get back to the casa before dark." He helped her into the vehicle, and then he swatted the horse on the rump and gave a shout. "Haw." She fought the horse to keep him in place.

"Why are you being so mean?" she demanded.

"Ask your papa." And he swatted the harnessed horse again. This time Cathy let the horse leave in a hurry and the wagon would slide on the turns.

"You were kind of hard on Miss Cathy," Chris said softly.

"Just following the patrons orders," Carlos said apologetically "nothing personal, amigo." Their eyes met for a few seconds.

"I know," Chris said.

"How is that black colt doing today?"

"He drank all the milk I had so I guess we need to milk a cow for more."

"That will be the day; I milk one of those long horns, just to feed that orphan."

"I'm an orphan too, just like Midnight." He snapped and walked toward the shack, past it then out to the corral. In a side pen to the barn the black colt whined at Chris' approach. "Don't tell me you're hungry again." The colt smelled at the hand of Chris as he patted the young horse on the nose.

"Chris," called Carlos as he approached the barn.

"Yes," replied Chris.

"Where have you been getting the milk for the colt?"

"I've milk a little from each of the mares."

"You what?"

"I am out of milk, now that all the nursing mares are out on the range."

"You're not suggesting we milk one of those longhorns?"

"Midnight still needs milk," Chris said soft and slowly "he not eating enough hay as yet."

"Amigo, that little horse is more trouble than he's worth," said Carlos.

"If you won't help me, then I'll just have to do it alone."

"Okay," I just hope Jefe don't catch wind of this."

§

"Here's my report on that skeleton that was found last month," said the doctor.

"It's about time," said the sheriff taking the file. "Now we can hold an inquest."

"It was the skeleton of a woman in her late twenties to early thirties. She stood about five foot four. She had reddish brown hair. She had no teeth, but she wore dentures. Her right leg had been broken at one time and it had healed, also her left arm. She at one time broke some ribs, which too had healed."

"You told me everything . . . except who she was."

"Well you didn't give me time," snapped the doctor. "I enquired among some of the doctors at the hospital. When I told them of my findings one of them . . . a Doctor Jarvis Larson told me of a patient of his who disappeared several years ago. He identified her as Mrs. Weston."

"So that's what happened to Barbara Weston," said the Sheriff.

"Not Barbara . . . she had a mouth full of teeth. It was the first wife of the Colonel, her name was Lucy. She lost her teeth when she was a young girl due to scurvy."

"You think the Colonel killed her and dumped her body in the swamp?"

"I don't know who killed her, but the cause of her death was a beating followed by a gunshot to the back of the head."

"Did you find the bullet?"

"No . . . unfortunately I did not."

"Looks like young Christopher Le Monte saved the tax payers the cost of a trial again."

"It would appear so."

"I wonder what Phillip and Bernie will have to say about Christopher, when I tell them we found their mother?" asked the Sheriff.

"That aught to be something to see," said the Doctor.

§

A lone cowboy, named Pete, was spotted riding hard and fast toward the main compound on the Morgan ranch. He rode right up to the back veranda and began to yell for John before the horse could stop running, he dismounted.

"What's all this?" shouted John.

"Its Chris," he staggered to the steps "He's been hurt and he's all busted up from tangling with a cow."

"Slowly, tell me what happened," said John. Betty and Cathy rushed to stand beside John.

"Chris needed milk for an orphan colt he's been raising, so he and Carlos roped a longhorn cow, so Chris could milk her," the cowboy said in strained breaths. "The cow kicked him than she stomped on him."

"How bad is he hurt?" Betty shouted.

"Is he still alive?" screamed Cathy.

"He was still in Texas when I left," replied Pete "how bad he's hurt, I don't know, but it look's real bad."

John helped the cowboy into a chair. He then turned to the ranch hands that gathered around to see what the trouble was all about.

"One of you men go to town and get the doctor," John directed. "You others get the buckboard hitched up and help get some blankets, pillows, food and water loaded." He then turned to the rider who brought the news. "Where's Chris now, at the remuda?"

"No, we thought we better not move him," the cowboy's voice was full of emotions. "Carlos and Bobby are with him near that far west hay field, and down along the stream just west a half mile."

"Near the big cottonwood tree?" asked John.

"The very spot."

"Okay, Pete you stay here and direct the doctor out to the area when he gets here." John rose up and watched as the buckboard was driven to the house. Betty, Cathy and two cowboys exited the house with their arms full of things that they thought they might need. All the items were placed on the wagon as John took inventory. "Listen up," he waited till he had every ones attention. "We may be there for a while, so you get the 'road gear,' tents and the chuck wagon and follow us. Now, you all know where we'll be, if any thing comes up. Everyone go on about your business and we will see you a day or two."

Cathy climbed aboard the wagon next to her mother.

"Cathy," John spoke affirmative to her, "you stay here."

"Like hell I will," she blurted out.

"John," Betty said "this is not the time, let her go."

"Oh hell, where's my horse?"

§

John rode up to the camp where Carlos and Bobby where keeping watch over Chris. He dismounted before the horse stopped moving. He ran to where Chris was laying on the ground. Carlos was kneeling beside Chris. He came to his feet and removed his hat, and holding it in front of him he began to speak. When the words did not come forth, he cleared his throat.

"Carlos," growled John "I aught-a . . ." he dropped to the ground. "Chris," he said softly and with deep affection. "Can you hear me son?"

"He's not said a word all day," the Mexican said.

"Chris, are you going to live?" John sobbed as he placed his hand on the boy's neck to feel for a pulse. He looked at the bloody patch of cloth on Chris' head, and then he moved his eyes to take in every inch of the lads' body. "Where's his boot?" he asked when he saw the right one missing from his foot.

"It's here," said Bobby.

Chris had been covered with a blanket; which John lifted to look at Chris' clothing. The left leg of his jeans was torn nearly off, and a big patch of bloody cloth was rapped around his left thigh, a little above the knee. John lowered the blanket slowly and relaxed into a setting position. He wiped his face with his handkerchief and blew his nose. Retuning the cloth to his pocket, he looked up at Carlos.

"Chris, he needed 'lache' for the 'potro' he's raising," Carlos said pleading his case.

"Didn't you give any thought at all, as to what might happen when milking a wild longhorn cow?

"Jefe it worked 'seis' times before."

"What? Six times before," John said loudly "Has every one on this ranch lost their minds."

About that time the buckboard arrived with the women. They too were very soon at Chris' side. Betty began to care for him as she washed the dirt away. Cathy let out a few sobs mixed with low voiced pleadings for the young man's life, as the tears rolled down her face. John rose and walked away with Carlos in tow as he pulled him along by his arm.

"Carlos," John spoke harshly then paused for a minute.

"Si, . . . Jefe, . . . me, I am sorry."

"You have a brain and you need to put it back into operation. If Chris needed milk for the colt then we have plenty at the house."

"Si . . . Jefe."

§

The doctor arrived with the chuck wagon two hours after the sun went into hiding for the night. Cookie set up camp and began to fix food and coffee for those gathered at the scene of the 'crime.' Doctor Corbin began his examination. It wasn't long before the MD had discovered most of his injuries.

"Well, he's got three broken ribs, a deep cut on his left thigh, a concussion which may have caused some brain damage, and lots of abrasions. I'm not too sure about his spine though. We need to get him off the ground and onto some thing warm and solid."

"How about the buckboard?" asked Betty "He will need to ride there back to the house, anyway?"

"Maybe in a day or two," said the MD "I need to be sure about his spine before we move him that far, so as soon as he wakes up, if ever." The doctor gathered every one around the youth and gave instructions as to how the lifting and placing of him onto the wagon should be done. Chris was then moved to the buckboard.

"Set up the tents," ordered John "looks like we are going to be here a spell." In the corner of his vision he caught sight of the very small horse coming into the camp. It made a straight line to where Chris was bedded on the wagon. He whinnied as he approached the injured and unconscious man. He whinnied again when the man did not respond. "Is that the runt, Chris risked his life for?"

"Si, Jefe," replied Carlos. "He is looking for his 'mama' to feed him."

"Take that . . . animal out and put it out of his misery."

"No, no Chris would kill me," cautioned Carlos "maybe anyone else."

"No daddy," yelled Cathy rushing to stand before her father "I'll take care of Chris' horse for him."

"Oh hell," John said disgusted "the whole world has gone insane."

§

90

Chris woke up two days later, just before noon. Doctor Corbin examined him and had him move his body slowly this way, that way, twist here and then there, up and down, over and around.

"His spine is fine, but his body is going to be sore for several weeks. He needs to stay in bed for at least three weeks. When he's able, he needs to walk, a little at first then increase the distance each day for two weeks. Those ribs will heal, but it will be two months, or more before he can go back to work, and then only light duty.

"We'll take good care of him," promised Betty. "He can sleep in the spare bedroom upstairs."

"No stairs," said the doctor.

"Well, he could sleep . . ." Betty didn't finish.

"He's going to sleep in my den," John said "then I can keep an eye on him."

"Humph," growled Cookie "when I got trampled by the team, they just threw me in the bunk house and said 'hurry up and get well." Every one laughed.

§

Chris became the patient living in John's study and office. John tried to make sure Cathy was never in the den at any time. But young people will always manage to get around the taboos parents put in place.

"Its time for Chris' lunch," said Betty as she loaded the tray of food. "John's out on the range, and now I need to go to town for some supplies."

"I'll take it in to him," said Cathy rising from the table. "I can eat my lunch with him."

"You know you father wouldn't stand for it."

"It won't take long for him to eat," she reasoned as she took hold of the try.

"I don't know," Betty said "if your father finds out, there will be hell to pay."

"What can it hurt for me to sit with Chris until he's through eating?" She asked. "When he's done then I'll clean up and bring the tray back to the kitchen."

"Well if you promise to come out as soon as Chris is finished eating,"

"Just as soon as Chris is done eating I will come right out," she promised.

Betty released her hold on the tray as Cathy took a firm grip of it.

"I shouldn't be more that two hours," said Betty. She took her light coat and sun bonnet from the hall tree and watched as her daughter entered the room where Chris was recuperating form the stomping the wild longhorn cow had given him. Betty sighed and then turned to leave the house. She walked to the barn to get the buckboard.

"Well, well what do we have here? Chris asked as she entered the room.

"I brought you your lunch," Cathy said sweetly.

"And now, what would you father say?" Chris said in a delighted tone of voice.

"He's out on the range and mother . . ."

"I heard, she's on her way to town."

"I can only stay until you are done eating so I can clear the tray out."

"In that case what if I take a bite every ten minutes or so?"

"Well that would be alright with me, but the food would get cold," she said.

"Okay, but don't ask me any questions about my past," he insisted.

"Not even about Louisiana?" she asked. "I've never been any where, why I've never been more that sixty miles from here."

"The vegetation changes, but the people never do."

"I hear that Louisiana is all green with lots of swamps . . . . . ."

Cathy would sneak in any time she could and the two would exchange little bits of their lives. She wanted to have Chris explain why he was supposed to be taboo. Chris would avoid any conversation that would lead up to the hidden secret.

The pair met any time they would be left alone in the house. Until one day as Chris was up and around. He was then to have his food at the table with the family. Then it was small talk, but lots of eyes between the two as they sat opposite at the table. When Chris was strong enough to take care of himself, he was moved to the bunk house. Cathy was devastated and she would make all kinds of excuses to visit the bunk-house. Chris was to feed the horses in the barn each day that way he could be with Midnight. Cathy had taken care of Midnight until Carlos took over and now it was up to Chris.

One day as they met in the barn while Chris was curing Midnight and rubbing him down. Cathy pushed too hard when she asked about the reason he was more or less hiding from the world.

"I want to know what happened that made you leave Louisiana?" she demanded.

"No, Cathy No," he said loudly in her face. He left Midnight in the stall and closed the gate. He then walked as fast as he could toward the main house. Cathy took a side door to the barn and circled around to the house. When she entered she could hear John in the kitchen. He was having a cup of coffee and a slice of apple pie.

"So you think you're ready to return to the remuda?" John asked.

"Yes sir, I am."

"What did the doctor say two days ago?" John asked. "As I recall he said light duty for another month. And you were to do those exercises he gave you."

Cathy started to enter the kitchen but stood in the doorway. Betty instantly saw the tears in her eyes. John had his back to her as he was seated at the table. He didn't see his daughter, but he knew by the expression on Chris' face that she was there. He sighed and laid down his fork on the partially eaten apple pie. He then placed his elbows on the table and cradled his head as he thought for an appropriate solution to this situation. Betty took Cathy by the arm and led her into the living room.

"I could just leave the ranch all together," said Chris.

"No Chris, you're not strong enough for that." He returned to his thought process. After a few minutes he raised his eyes to meet with those of Chris.

"Son, the only way I see it . . . in the morning I will take you out to the remuda. There's not much you can do out there but Carlos will find some thing to keep you busy."

"That will be alright," said Chris.

"No Chris," said John "It's not alright for any of the parties involved."

"John one day soon I'll have to leave."

"I know," said John as the sorrow grew in his chest. He knew that one day there would be a parting of those involved. He hoped that day would never come.

§

"It's been three years," screamed Phillip at his brother and Choctaw Charlie "and you haven't found hide, nor hair of him yet. What the hell have you two been doing?"

"It's as if the earth just opened and swallowed him up," said Bernie.

"I've been to every town and ranch in the Pecos area . . . nobody has seen him," said Charlie.

"Could he have gone to California . . . or Oregon . . . how about the moon . . . you two couldn't find a feather in a chicken pen?" Phillip waved his hands skyward in the Dallas Hotel room. "Do I have to do it for you?"

"He'll show up . . . sooner or later, Phil," said Bernie.

"Well . . . now it's later . . . so where the hell is he? . . . dear brother and don't call me Phil." Bernie shrugged his shoulders with his hands out stretched.

"Maybe, if we were to increase the reward?" asked Bernie.

"To what?" asked Phillip?

"How about four thousand dollars?" Bernie suggested.

"That would get quick results," Charlie said, all excited at the prospects of so much money.

"Okay . . . we'll get them to run a story in the newspapers about wanting to find our long lost brother . . . to give him his share in the estate of our late father," suggested Phillip "that aught to smoke the rat out of his hole."

§

"Daddy there's a dance at the town hall in Willow Bend next Saturday night," Cathy said at the supper table one night.

"You want to go . . . I suppose," he winked at his wife setting next to him at the small table.

"I would . . . only . . . I don't have a date."

"Well . . . I'm not going to take you to the dance either," he smiled "I promised I'd take your mother."

"I was thinking . . . why you don't nudge . . . Chris into taking me?" she asked.

"I told you to leave him out of your life," said John firmly, but lovingly "he's got something on his mind and only he can solve it."

"Is that why for the past three year you never let him around the ranch house, except when he was hurt? You always keep him out on the range, or out in the line shacks . . . I don't get to see him very often and when I do, he avoids me."

"I told you he has a problem to solve . . . so leave him be," said John sternly.

"Mother . . . my I be excused?" she snapped.

"Of coarse you may dear." The young girl ran from the room and out into the night air. "John . . . I know the real reason . . . but don't you think it's about time she knew the truth about Chris?"

"I should have never brought him here," he said as he placed his face into his hands for a second to rub his face. "Chris has been like the son we never had, but there is going be real trouble for anyone around him and I don't want Cathy to get mixed up in it."

"Of coarse you should have brought him here, it was the Christian thing to do, Dear, he needed help and he's a real nice young man now," said his wife. "Now you tell her the truth about Chris . . . then you leave the rest up to her."

"Maybe your right," he said "I'll have a long talk with her in the morning.

§

Cathy walked around the ranch compound for more than a half hour. In the corral she noticed a lone figure of a man seated on one end of the watering trough. As she slowly drew closer she recognized it was Chris.

"Hello," she called to him as she climbed the corral fence to set on the top rail.

"Hello yourself," he replied as he turned to face her. He rose from his seat on the tank and removed his hat.

"What are you doing out here this time of night?" she asked.

"Miss Cathy . . . would you believe that I was holding this water tank down so it wouldn't run away?"

"I don't think so," she replied "anyway . . . it's got too much water to move."

"It does . . . I hadn't noticed."

"There's something else you haven't noticed," she said climbing down the fence on his side and stepping closer to him.

"Oh . . . what's that?" he asked.

"Me."

"Miss Cathy . . . I promised your father that I wouldn't . . ." she cut him off.

"Me, damn it, me, not daddy, not mother, me." Her voice was elevated to near yelling.

"I can't . . . you won't like what you'll find and beside you deserve much better" he said and quickly walked to the gate. He mounted his horse and rode away at a full gallop.

John heard her yelling and he came to investigate. "What's all the commotion about?" He found her in the corral in tears which she wiped away when she saw him coming inside the enclosure.

"Chris . . . he ran away from me." She placed her hands to her face and sobbed. John took his daughter in his arms, but she pushed him away and ran to the house. He could see the dust lingering in the air that Chris's horse, Midnight now full grown, had stirred up. John quickly saddled another horse and took out after him.

Chris pulled up to a hitching rail in the nearby town of Willow Bend. The hitching rail was in front of the Silver Dollar Saloon. Inside were a dozen, or more cowboys, three females, the bar tender, and one old piano player. He was busy pounding out a tune on the worn and beaten old 88. Chris didn't stop to read the room like he usually did, this time he went straight to the bar. He ordered whiskey and the barman set a glass in front of him and then poured the glass full. He started to take the bottle away.

"Leave it," said Chris sharply. He then threw a folded five dollar bill on the bar. The bartender took the bill to make change while Chris drank the liquid down then to pour one more.

"Well now . . . what do we have here?" said a coarse voice behind him.

Chris looked up into the mirror behind the bar. Standing behind him about ten feet away was a medium sized man dressed in tight jeans, blue bibbed shirt, boots half way to his knees with a bowie knife stuffed in one, a red bandana around his neck and a tan colored Stetson hat on his back, held there by the black cord around his neck. On each hip he wore a pistol in cut down holsters. It was plain to see this fellow was a gunman and he was spoiling for a fight.

"No," said Chris as he pushed the bottle and glass aside. "I don't want any trouble tonight . . . I just want a drink, or two."

"You yellow . . . or something?" said the man.

"I guess I am," said Chris.

"I think you're more then yellow . . . maybe even a mama's boy?"

"What ever you say," said Chris. He still had his back to the man and his eyes on the mirror.

"Damn it boy . . . what does it take to get you riled?"

John stepped to the saloon door and placed his hand on one of the bat wing doors. He stood there watching.

"I just want a drink," said Chris.

"I aint never shot anyone in the back before . . . so you's best turn around."

"I am going to stay this way."

"Well now . . . maybe you should . . . after all it's only fittin' to shoot cowards in the back."

"I don't want to fight you," said Chris "I'm tired of killing."

"What've you been killin'. . . boy . . . rats?"

"Yeah . . . come to think of it . . . they were all rats . . . just like you."

The man's face hardened and his lips closed tightly then he drew one revolver and fired in the direction of Chris. At the same time Chris twisted to one side as he drew his gun and fired at the man. The gunman staggered back, and then pointed his gun at Chris again to fire once more. Chris fired twice more at the man and this time the man went down to the floor. Chris grabbed the edge of the bar to sturdy himself. There was blood coming from his shirt just under his right arm. John raced forward and took hold of him.

"You alright?" asked John.

"Yeah, it's just a flesh wound . . . damn it sure hurts," Chris growled.

"A few inches to the left and he'd a killed you," said John.

"I think maybe it's time I got me a bigger gun," said Chris "I hit him all three times."

"I was hoping it was time you threw away that gun and became respectable," said John. "Besides, Cathy has taken a shine to you."

Chris looked him in the face and pushed him away. "I never had the chance . . . and you know it . . . and now . . . I guess I never will." He started to the door.

"Mister," called the barman "your change."

"Keep it for the mess I caused."

"You didn't, it was that idiot that caused it."

"You tell it that way . . . if and when you're asked," said John as he followed Chris out the door.

"Let's go to the house and fix that up," said John.

"You go home to your family," said Chris as he mounted and pulled Midnight to stand still in the road. "Me . . . I'm heading out."

"Chris . . . you can't," pleaded John.

"Can't . . . I must . . . this time tomorrow the whole country will know where I am. So . . . like it or not . . . I must. I never wanted to cause you, or Betty . . . and now (choke) Cathy any trouble."

John shook his head and raised his hand to shake Chris' hand. "Drop me a line now and then . . . let me know how you're doing . . . Chris . . . please . . . stay alive."

"I'll do my best . . . one day at a time," said Chris as he pulled Midnight toward the street. "You told me one time, I could have one of the horses when I quit, may I keep Midnight?"

"He's yours, in more ways then one."

Chris gave a sloppy salute and said "so long."

§

"Phil," screamed Bernie as he came bursting into the room.

"Don't call me Phil," shouted Phillip "my name it PHILLIP. Now what is it?" He was seated at the table in their home having his morning meal.

"He's back," said Bernie holding out the newspaper. "It says he shot it out with a man in . . aww . . . here it is . . . Willow Bend Texas . . . that's in the Pecos country."

"So the little Bastard . . . is still alive, is he," said Phillip as he scanned the folded paper. "Get your suit case . . . you're going back to Texas and I'm coming too, this time we're going to find him."

§

Chris rode south from Willow bend for two days. He avoided any-one he saw along the way. On the third day he came across a wagon all painted with scenes of people handling snakes, facing lions, shooting at things in the air and others throwing knifes. The wagon was stuck in some mud at a crossing of a low running stream. A man was trying to remove some mud from around one of the wheels as Chris rode up to the wagon.

"You need some help?" he asked.

99

"You're dern tootin' . . . she's in too deep for my old horse." He stood erect; his hands were covered in mud. He attempted to step out of the mire and nearly lost his balance as he pulled one foot out to take a step toward dry land. Then he almost did it again with the other foot. Twice more and then once more he was on firm dry ground. Chris rode around to the front of the wagon and saw the old mare almost up to her belly in mud and water.

"If you try to go forward any more . . . you'll just get in deeper," explained Chris as he surveyed the situation. "Best to unhitch your horse and then we'll use both horses to pull the wagon back out of there."

"Okay," said the man as he waded back out to do as Chris had suggested. Once the mare was released from the wagon the man whipped her up and guided her to the rear of the wagon. "What now?"

"Attach the 'traces' to the wagon frame and tie the end of my rope there too." The man did as he was instructed and then they used both horses to pull the wagon. It took a couple of attempts to rock the wagon free of the muck. It then came back slowly onto dry ground.

"Worked like a charm," shouted the man "thanks Mister." He untied the rope and the traces to his mare. He then drove her around to the front and was about to hitch her up to it once more.

"Why don't you make camp on this side of the river," asked Chris "that old mare could use some rest . . . and looks like she could use lots of feed to boot."

"I think your right," he said. "Let me clean some of this mud off my person then I'll cook you the biggest, tastiest, thickest pot of beans you ever did partake of in all your born days."

"If, you are inviting me, to stay for supper, I except?"

"Don't know what else I was ah doing . . . It'll take me a few minutes . . . be right back." He ran down to the rivers edge and waded into the rushing water. There he washed away the mud. He then came and drove the mare into the stream and washed her and the harness clean of mud. When he returned to the wagon he removed the harness and taking a long rope he tied one end to the mare's neck then the other end to a log in the middle of some green grass. "There you go Mert, eat your fill." He walked back to the wagon. Chris had removed his saddle and placed it on an old log, and then turned Midnight loose to graze on the grass. "My handle is Professor McKnight . . . I've been everywhere

. . . west of the Mississippi . . . seen more wonders then you can shake a stick at . . . loved more women . . . shot more bull . . . so on and so forth. Really, I'm just one old tired and weary snake oil peddler . . . just call me Professor." He held out his hand and they shook.

"Christopher Le Monte . . . just call me Chris."

"Chris . . . my friend, there is nothing better than a good pot of beans to keep one well fed . . . that is unless you happen to have a couple of 'T' bone steaks. I like mine rare on the inside and brown on the outside."

Chris shook his head in the negative "I don't have any supplies with me . . . I sort of left very sudden like . . . back there."

"Are you running, from something . . . or someone . . . the law perhaps?"

"Not the law . . . just two . . . or it could be . . . three men."

"I see . . . well one good turn deserves another . . . so let's eat first . . . then we'll discuss . . . your situation later. You gather some wood for a fire, while I find a couple a cans of beans. Ah, say did you know your horse is loose?"

"He won't go far," mused Chris "he thinks I'm his mama."

"You will definitely have to explain that one to me."

"What is all this?" asked Chris as he waved his hand toward the wagon.

"I travel from town to town peddling my wondrous and amazing Cherokee Snake Oil. It cures the . . ." he went into his spiel but stopped and lowered his voice "it won't cure a damn thing. It's just alcohol with a few other things thrown in to confuse the taste buds in ones mouth. I normally charge the 'Mark' one dollar for eight ounces of this stuff. It will only make them high for a little while. However there are some, who, for some strange reason, or other, claimed to have been cured of a host of ailments. But don't ask me why." He pulled the cork on the bottle he was holding and took a long drink then threw the empty bottle into the wagon. He then pulled another one from his coat and removed the stopper. "Care to join me in a little lavation?"

Chris shook his head negatively "The last time I took a drink . . . a man was killed."

"By you . . . I suppose."

"Yes . . . by me."

"Did he need killing?"

"How do I answer that question . . . I don't know?"

"What happened . . . if you don't mind my asking?"

"He goaded me into drawing," said Chris "and he nearly killed me." He opened his shirt to show the wound on his side.

"That looks bad. When's the last time that was cleaned and dressed?"

"It's just a scratch."

"It looks infected to me. Better let me clean and dress it for you . . . or it'll get a lot worse."

"Maybe I'll have some of that snake oil. You think it might just cure it for me?"

"Only, if you were to pour it on the wound."

§

Early in the morning Chris checked his ammo supply in the gun-belt and saddle bags. Thirty rounds were all he had left. He decided to just practice his draw that day and save the bullets for later. He was whipping the pistol out as fast as he could and stopping just short of pulling the trigger on his target.

Professor McKnight climbed down the wagon steps, and then stretched his arms and body to shake off the sleep. He watched as Chris drew and pointed the gun at a can setting on a log several feet in front of him.

"Can you hit it?" he asked as he walked up behind Chris.

Chris drew and fired a round to hit the can dead center. It flew away from him to land in the dirt. He drew and hit it again and it moved further away. A third time he drew and hit it again to send it rolling along for a few more feet.

"Nicely done," the Professor said "who ever taught you sure knew his business."

"Amanbythenameof BuckyMorse," saidChris. "HelivesinfarEastTexas."

"Bucky Morse . . . now that's a name I haven't heard in a long time," he said sadly.

"You know him . . . don't you?"

"I did know him, darn good friend," the Professor said with his head and voice lowered.

"What, he's dead?"

"He was killed a short while back," he said lowly "someone stabbed him while he slept in his bed."

"Choctaw Charlie . . . that no good half breed," said Chris.

"No, no Charlie's a good friend of Bucky's," protested the Professor.

"Not when it came to the bounty on my head," said Chris "I should have killed him instead of shooting the knife out of his hand, and Bucky said so."

"I see. Say just how long are you going to continue to use that pea shooter?"

"Bucky started me with this thirty eight because I was only six-teen at the time."

"Well, you're not a little boy any more . . . it's time you had a real man's gun."

"You may be right . . . but I don't see any gun shops around here."

"I have been saving one for someone special . . . Bucky turned it down several years back," said the Professor as he walked toward the wagon and climbed the steps. He went inside and a few minutes later he came back out. In his hands was a walnut case with the gold figure of a rearing horse, the emblem of the Colt Firearms Company. He opened the case to reveal a Nickel plated, engraved, and Ivory gripped Colt .45 Peace Maker Model. He handed the case to Chris.

"That is sure one fine piece of artery," said Chris "but it should rightly belong to someone who would use it to help people in distress . . . not a wanted man like me."

"Who says you're wanted? The law, or them two half brothers of yours?" snapped the professor. "Seams to me you need to stand up to them and stop your running away."

"I don't want to fight with them," said Chris softly.

The Professor snapped the lid shut on the case and said "Then run like a coward." He took the box from Chris's hands and started to walk away.

"What about other men … like the one's I've killed in those saloon fights?"

"There are always going to be thugs and no goods that will oppress the weak," said the Professor as he stopped and turned to face Chris. "You are right this gun should only be used to protect those who are being oppressed."

"That's a tall order … for someone who's only twenty one years old."

"It's a tall order for anyone … no matter their age." The Professor came back to stand before Chris. He once more opened the box. "Take the gun and take the challenge."

§

"I don't know how so many people in one town never heard of the shooting that took place here," roared Phillip as him and his brother stood on the board walk of Willow Bend Texas.

"Phil," said Bernie "I found one who heard of a shooting about ten years ago … but that was in El Paso."

"Stop calling me Phil. Wonder if Charlie has found out anything?" asked Phillip. "Here he comes now." The Indian strolled up to them. "Did you find out anything?"

"Sure did," he said and took them by the arms to pull them to one side, so anybody walking past would not be able to over hear their conversations. "I found the town drunk out behind the Silver Dollar Saloon … and he remembered three weeks ago there was a shooting in the saloon. A Mexican dressed all in black shot and killed a bad man named Terry Blankenship … he had a reputation for being a fast gun … but this other fellow shot him three times and killed him."

"We're not looking for a Mexican … we're looking for a Cajun," said Phillip loudly.

"Hold your voice down," said Charlie "I could pass for a Mexican and so could Christopher Le Monte."

"Oh, okay . . . I'll go a long with that . . . but why doesn't anyone want to talk about it?"

"John Morgan, he's one of the biggest ranchers around here and he's very well liked by one and all . . . it was his idea for everyone to keep quiet about the shooting to strangers."

"So where did he go after the shooting?" asked Bernie.

"The old drunk, said he rode south out of town, even after John Morgan begged him to stay."

"South huh . . . what's south of here?"

"There is a lot of open country between here and Mexico," said Charlie.

"There's got to be ranches and towns out there . . . somewhere," said Bernie.

"Well . . . let's head south and start asking questions on the way to Mexico."

§

Laredo Texas was a sleepy little town near the boarder with Mexico. Largely built of adobe bricks and plastered with white stucco. Main Street was wide and almost deserted at noon time as the hot sun beat down. In one of the cantinas, someone was playing a Spanish flamenco tune on a guitar. Chris rode past the building and stopped several yards further up the street. He brought his horse to a halt near a tank filled with water for livestock. At one end sat a hand pump. He placed his hands on the pump and worked the handle several times. When the water began to run, he quickly removed his hat and placed his head under the flow of cool water. The shock of cold to his hot body made him shiver for a few seconds.

The Professor parked the wagon at the water trough, so his mare could drink. He then dismounted the highly painted cart and tied the lead rope to the hitching post.

"I could use a cold drink myself," said the Professor looking all around.

"The water's clear and cold," said Chris as he began to work the handle once more.

"That stuff's for horses, cows, pigs and goats. What I need is a tall glass of ice cold beer . . . followed by a glass filled with Bourbon."

"Okay," said Chris "you go to the Cantina and I'll take care of the horses."

"Thanks my friend," and off trotted the Professor to disappear from Chris's view into the building. Inside he went straight to the bar. On his way he passed lots of tables, which were empty. Off to the right was a low stage where sat a Mexican on a stool, he had been playing the guitar. He stopped when the Professor came through the door. His eyes followed him to the bar. On the left, a lone man was seated at a table. He was eating some beans and tortillas. He had a bottle of Tequila and a glass half full of the booze in front of him. He too, kept his eyes on the Professor.

"Barman . . . a tall cold beer and a shot of Bourbon if you please?" ordered the Professor to the fat chubby Mexican bartender.

"Thee beer . . . she is not too cold senior," he replied.

"Whatever," said the Professor "Just make it a tall one."

"Si, Senior." The barman worked the tap to draw a thick headed glass full, then past it across the bar to the Professor. He took the glass and placing it to his lips and began to gulp the contents down. He didn't halt until the glass was drained to where there was less than an inch of beer left.

"Aawww," exclaimed the Professor setting the glass on the bar and wiping the foam from his upper lip. "Well." He said looking the barman in the eye.

"Well, what senior?" asked the barman.

"My good man . . . where is my shot of Bourbon?"

"I am sorry senior . . . we have no . . . how you say . . . Bur-ban . . . only Tequila."

"Close enough." The barman quickly set a glass on the bar and poured it to the rim with the clear liquid from a bottle. The Professor tipped it up and swallowed the entire contents of the glass. "Ooowe . . . that's just like cleaning fluid."

"Professor," said the lone man seated at a corner table. He turned toward the voice. It took a few seconds for him to recognize the man now walking toward him.

"Choctaw Charlie . . . I do believe," said the Professor in a very loud voice. Charlie looked surprised at the elevated tone he used to greet him. Charlie held out his hand as he got closer to him.

"It's been a long time," said Charlie.

"It certainly has been a long time, Choctaw Charlie." This time his words were even louder.

"What's with you?" asked Charlie.

"Nothing," said the Professor. He pulled a silver coin from his pocket and tossed it to the barman. "Will that cover my bill?"

"Si Senior."

"I think I better hit the road," said the Professor as he started toward the door.

"I'll walk out with you," said Charlie.

"That won't be necessary . . . I can find my way to the door."

"Something's wrong . . . what is it?"

"Not a thing . . . I have to leave town . . . the sooner the better." He pulled away from Charlie and hurried to the door way. "It's been nice seeing you Choctaw Charlie," he shouted loudly. This time Chris heard the cry and he quickly tied his horse to the wheel of the wagon. He came closer and stood near the wooden walk way. The Professor came out and went straight to the middle of the street with Charlie following close behind him.

"Hello Charlie," said Chris standing to his left. Charlie jumped when he heard his name called. He became really nervous, when he realized who it was that had called his name. "Bucky called you his friend . . . he also said I should have killed you when I had the chance."

"Christopher Le Monte," he said and lifted his hands into the air "Please . . . don't kill me . . . I beg you." He began to walk slowly backwards down the street; Chris matched his pace step for step.

"Did Bucky beg for his life . . . or did you just stab him in the back while he slept?"

"Please . . . don't."

"You're just plain yellow . . . the only way you could have done it was in the back."

"If you don't kill me . . . I'll tell you about those two brothers of yours." His voice was shaky as he pleaded.

"There's a jail right behind you," said Chris "drop your weapons and go inside."

"Your brothers . . . they'll get you . . . if you don't let me help you."

"You . . . help me . . . just like you helped Bucky?" Chris stopped walking toward Charlie "Drop your weapons, or draw . . . damn you."

Charlie's hands went to his belt buckle which he unfastened and dropped the belt and its load of weapons which fell to the ground. "Don't shoot . . . I give up."

"Inside the jail," ordered Chris. The half Indian turned with his hands in the air and walked to the jail house. He went through the door and quickly stepped to one side. He was now out of Chris's sight. He drew a small gun from his boot. He cocked the weapon and pointed it chest high at the open door way. He stood there for several seconds until his name was called again.

"Charlie . . . what do you think you're doing?" asked Chris from outside the jail. "Either you step back into view, or I'll shoot you on sight."

"Chris . . . let me go and I'll help you with your brothers."

"What kind of a fool do you take me for . . . Charlie? You killed Bucky . . . so now you're going to pay for it . . . as for my so called brothers . . . . I don't need any help with them."

Charlie looked around the office of the jail. His eye caught the shotgun in a rack on the wall behind the desk. He jumped over the desk and grabbed it. He had trouble with the locking mechanism that held the weapon in the rack. He was still trying to free the gun from the rack, when Chris entered the jail. He began to laugh when he saw Charlie struggled to free the weapon. Charlie pulled the derringer from his waist band and pointed it at Chris. Seeing him drawing the little gun, Chris exited the building.

"You better give up Charlie," yelled Chris as he stood close to the wall beside the door.

Charlie retuned to the shotgun once more and shouted "Never."

Just then a man came running toward the jail house. On his chest was a badge which had sheriff inscribed on it. "What's going on here?" he demanded with his gun drawn. Chris raised his hands to shoulder height.

"This half breed killed a friend of mine in the eastern part to the state," explained Chris. "I was just trying to get him to surrender to the law."

"Who are you to be capturing anyone?" demanded the Sheriff.

"Nobody . . . just the friend of the man he killed by stabbing him in the back."

"Okay . . . you stay right here and let me handle this," ordered the man.

"He's all yours," said Chris as he stepped away from the door. "I should tell you this . . . he's trying to get your shotgun out of the rack . . . oh yeah . . . one more thing . . . he's got a derringer in his waist band." Chris walked away from the jail and toward his horse. He untied the animal and walked back toward the jail, he stopped and waited about twenty yards from the jail house.

"You, in the Jail . . . this is the Sheriff," he yelled as he stood next to the door way. "Give yourself up and you won't be harmed."

"Okay," said Charlie. A few seconds went by.

"Step into the door way so I can see you," demanded the Sheriff.

"My hand is caught," Charlie said.

"Okay . . . I'm coming in," he said and stepped into the door way.

"NO!" Screamed Chris as the man stepped into the open door way. There was a loud blast as the shotgun fired and knocked the man backwards out into the street. Chris drew his gun and ran forward to the door way. There he stood for a second then peeked inside. Charlie was trying to get the shotgun reloaded. "Charlie" he shouted. The Indian dropped the shotgun and tried to draw his little gun. He cocked it and pointed it at Chris. There was the sound of a very loud blast from the .45 in Chris's hand. The bullet hit Charlie in the heart and he fell backwards onto the floor.

Lots of people gathered round the jail house as Chris walked to his horse and mounted. He pulled his stud over to the Professor. "It never stops."

"No . . . my friend . . . and possibly it never will."

"So long," said Chris as he waved a two finger salute to the Professor and pulled Midnight around.

"Goodbye, my friend . . . stay alive."

§

"Charlie's dead," yelled Bernie as he came rushing into the hotel room in Odessa.

"What?" said Phillip seated in a bath tub in the middle of the floor. Bernie shoved the newspaper under his nose and pointed to the article.

Choctaw Charlie a Half Breed Indian of Louisiana shot and killed the Sheriff of Laredo and seconds later he in turn was gunned down by an unidentified lone Gunman. The scene of the shooting took place in the office of the Sheriff of Laredo as he was trying to arrest Choctaw Charlie on a charge of murder which took place in East Texas. The lone gunman was dressed in black and carried a very fancy revolver. He rode out of town before anyone could get his name. The Texas Rangers are looking into the matter.

"I don't believe it," roared Phillip as he stood to get out of the tub. Bernie handed him a bath towel which he ignored. "This is outrageous," he yelled as he began to pace the floor. Bernie kept trying to give him the towel. "How long are the authorities going to allow this murderer to roam free?"

"You need this, Phil," begged Bernie holding out the towel.

"What I need is to get my hand's on Christopher Le Monte . . . that's what I need, and don't call me Phil." He started to open the door to the hall way.

"Stop," shouted Bernie.

"What on earth for?" asked Phillip annoyed with his brother.

"For this," he held up the towel once more "and your clothes," he explained.

Phillip looked down, suddenly he realized he was dressed only in his . . . birthday suite. He went quickly to the tub and climbed back into the water. "This bath cost me two dollars so I better get my money's worth out of it."

"Right, Phil," said Bernie with a sigh.

"And don't call me Phil," he demanded loudly.

§

A lone figure in the pouring rain rode across the open field toward the ranch house. John Morgan was seated on the covered veranda with his good friend U S Senator McWilliams from Houston. The two men were discussing everything under the sun, except politics. John watched the rider making his way toward him. When he was about thirty yards away John quickly jumped to his feet and went to the screened door of the porch.

"Chris . . . is that you?" he called out only to be drowned out by a clap of thunder. He called again "Chris."

"Hi John . . . may I stay awhile on your land?"

"Come in out of that rain," shouted John. Chris dismounted and walked to the porch steps. Located at the corner of the covered porch a small stream of rainwater poured into a barrel already full.

"I got several men after me," said Chris as he stood on the rain soaked ground.

John's wife Betty came to the door to look out at Chris. She called his name

111

"Chris . . . don't just stand there . . . please son, come in out of the rain." He climbed the steps to enter the door and once he was out of the rain he removed his hat.

"Mrs. Morgan," he said "It's a real pleasure seeing you once more, ma'am." A flash of lighting was quickly followed by a very loud clap of thunder.

"What's wrong, some men following you?" asked John.

"About two dozen, maybe more in a posse, have been tracking me for the past week. I've tried every thing I know to shake them off my trail, but they just keep coming."

"Chris," Betty asked "when's the last time you had a decent meal?"

"The last time I was here . . . ma'am."

"Take off those wet clothes . . . John, get him something to wear . . . then you come into the kitchen and I'll have a hot meal for you." She hurried to the kitchen.

"I don't want to bring any trouble to your door," said Chris as he looked into the face of his old boss and good friend. "Midnight is worn out, so may I trade for a fresh horse? I don't want to lose Midnight and he'll be at home here."

"You don't have to ask me that, you take what ever you need. Well, you better get out of those wet clothes and into some dry ones, or the wife will skin me alive," the three men laughed. Chris began to remove his outer garments and John went inside the house.

"I don't believe I've had the pleasure," said the senator as he removed himself from his chair and came to shake hands with Chris. "I'm Senator Bryan McWilliams from Houston."

"Christopher Le Monte," he took the hand and they shook.

"Not thee Le Monte . . . that's been killing men in every corner of the state?" The senator looked horrified.

"I can't deny it," said Chris as he watched the man's face.

"Here you go Chris," said John when he returned after a minute or two. He handed him a towel to dry with. The dry clothes he held in his other hand. Chris had stopped removing his wet things and was now standing looking at the two men before him.

"Well . . . come on . . . get out of those wet things," ordered John.

"I shouldn't have come here," said Chris "your friends may not approve of me, so I just better ride on." He turned toward his horse.

"What's this?" John said loudly "Who won't approve of you coming here?"

"Him," Chris said as he pointed with his thumb back toward the senator.

"Wait a minute," ordered John "Chris you change your clothes and go have that meal." He then turned to face the Senator. "Sir, you and I must have a long talk in my study." He pointed the way. "There're some things you need to know." They both went inside the house. Chris dried himself and changed into the dry clothing. He then went into the house and walked into the kitchen. He went to the cook stove to warm himself for a few moments.

"How'd you like your eggs?" Betty asked, she was busy with a large skillet

"However you fix them will be just fine with me," he replied.

"You set down and drink this coffee," she said pouring a cup full, and then set the cup on the table in front of him. "I'll have your steak done in a jiffy."

"Thank you Mrs. Betty," he said and returned her smile. She returned to the stove and flipped the eggs. She took a platter and placed a very large steak on it. Then she scooped up the four eggs from the skillet and placed then on top of the meat. After taking a baked potato from the warming bin, she then placed the dish in front of Chris.

"If that's not enough . . . you just say so and I'll fix you some more."

"I don't know if I can eat all this," he said jokingly.

"Well, you do the best you can." She patted him on the shoulder. "How nice it is to see you again." She poured herself a cup of coffee, set some bread on the table and then took a seat next to him. He started to rise, but she stopped him. "Keep your seat."

"Yes, Mrs. Betty,"

"John's been worried sick about you for the past two years now, he keeps saying, where's Chris?" She watched as he ate his food. "Cathy wanted to say goodbye when you left."

"I didn't treat her right . . . for that I am truly sorry, Miss Betty."

"All of it wasn't your fault . . . there's blame enough to go around," she patted him on the arm. "She's at the neighbors, but she'll be home tomorrow and I know she'd be pleased to see you again."

"I can't stay that long," said Chris "I need a change of horses, and then I'll be on my way."

"She won't understand a second time," said Betty.

"I don't want to bring my trouble down on you," he said "so I'll have to be gone before sunrise."

"Chris, who's chasing you?" asked John standing at the kitchen door.

"The Westons," he replied "They've gathered a bunch of bounty hunters to help track me down."

"I explained everything to the senator about you and you're brothers," said John "he's agreed to help you settle this with them once and for all."

"Who's he going to have shot?" asked Chris in a huff "me, or them?"

"Neither . . . my boy," said the senator pushing past John and coming into the room. "Betty my dear, do you have any of that lovely coffee left?"

"I sure do," She rose from her chair "you set down and I'll pour you a big cup full."

"I'm sorry I took offence at you Chris . . . . John explained every-thing. You see all I've ever heard was your brother's side of the story. Now I understand your side. When I get back to Washington I'm going to raise all kinds of . . . excuse me Betty . . . hell with the Justice Depart-ment and the office of the U S Marshall."

"That still won't stop them," said Chris "they have sworn to kill me and that's the only thing they have on their minds."

"How old are you, my boy?" asked the Senator.

"Don't call me that again," said Chris angrily.

"Oh! Yeah, I forgot . . . I mean no disrespect," said the Senator.

"I told you he's a full gown man now," said John.

"I apologize too senator," said Chris "I shouldn't be so sensitive . . . especially around . . . my friends. I turned twenty three last month."

"Then I hope you will count me among your friends," said the senator. He held out his hand. Chris took it and they shook once more.

"Yes, Senator . . . you're right near the top."

"Mama . . . I'm home," shouted Cathy as she burst into the house. She ran for the back of the house and into the kitchen. Her mother was not there so she turned to the stairway. "Mama," she called again.

"I'm up here, dear," her mother called. Cathy climbed the steps leading to the second floor in a real big hurry.

"Oh, mama, guess what?" she said all excited.

"My, my, what's all the fuss?" asked her mother.

"Darin Keys has asked me to marry him," said Cathy.

"Wonderful," said her mother in an unexcited way.

"Mama did you hear me . . . Darin asked me to marry him?"

"Yes Dear . . . I heard you."

"What's the matter . . . I thought you'd be as excited as I am?"

"There's someone with your father," Betty was struggling to find the right words to tell her daughter.

"I know . . . its Senator McWilliams," she replied.

"No . . . well yes . . . but some one else is with him," she couldn't find the words "They're out in the barn."

"Who, mama?"

"You best, go see for yourself, dear."

"I bet it's Aunt Polly," she said and ran down the steps and out into the yard. She was still running when she came into the barn. She came to a halt when she saw Chris saddling a sorrow gelding, and standing near by was the senator and her father. "Chris," she gasped.

He stood looking at her and his feelings began to get all mixed up together. He wanted to leave, but then he wanted to stay. He wanted her to stay, but then he wanted her to leave. He removed his hat and held it in front of him, as if it would shield him so she would not be able to see him anymore.

"Miss Cathy," he said with a strained voice.

"Cathy, my dear," said the senator as he started to walk forward. John took him by the arm and led him in the opposite direction. "What?"

"I have a very fine horse you have just got to see," said John as he held his index finger to his lips. "He's outside here." They continued to walk away from the two left in the barn.

"You're looking ... fine," she said and slowly took two steps closer.

"You look ... terrific," he said and took a step closer.

"Do I ... really," she said and again slowly took two more steps.

"I'm sorry for the way I left," he said but took no more steps.

"Daddy told me everything," she said and took another step.

"I have to leave again," he said and took a step backwards.

"You do ... why?" she took a step back.

"I'm being hunted by a pack of bounty hunters the Weston's hired," he said and took three steps back.

"Chris," she said as a tear ran down her cheek "please ... don't go."

"I have to ... or there could be trouble for all of you." He turned his back, took a step then stopped. "When it over ... may I come back?"

"No!" she said firmly, and then she began to cry "If you leave now .... I'll be married in a month."

He turned to face her once more. "Congratulations ... who's the lucky guy?"

"It could be you ... if you'd stay," she sobbed.

His brain was filled with wild thoughts as he looked at her standing there with tears streaming down her face. In his mind the sound of gunshots, the number of men falling before him in all the gun fights smeared the pleasant thoughts all red with their blood.

"Cathy ... you know there is going to be more blood spilled," he said "do you want me to stay knowing it could be mine?"

"If you take off that gun," she reasoned "then there would be no more blood shed."

"It's not me," he said "It's my brothers."

"We'll just let the law take care of them," she wiped at her tears.

"There's no chance of that," said a voice from the door way beside her. Chris looked over to see the man entering the barn with his pistols drawn and cocked. "I got a message for you . . . it's from Phillip and Bernie."

"I can guess what it says," said Chris with his hands lifted to shoulder height.

"I just bet you can," said the man. "Right now I'm the lucky one, that's my name, 'Lucky' and I'm a bounty hunter."

"I'm not wanted by the law," said Chris.

"That don't matter none to me," said Lucky "your brothers have offered $4,000 for your head . . . now the problem is . . . if I kill you . . . I have to face the law . . . but if I hold you until they arrive . . . they kill you, then they have to face the law . . . and me . . . well that $4,000 will keep me in senioritis and Tequila for a long, long time."

"You're an animal," Cathy said in a nasty tone.

"I may be sweetheart, but then you see I'm the one holding all the Aces."

"What now?" Chris asked.

"You're brothers will be here shortly," he replied "I sent my, so called partner to fetch them."

"I see," said Chris. "Cathy . . . do you still want me to stay?"

"Yes . . . more than anything," she said and started to walk toward him.

"Hold it," ordered Lucky. He moved both guns toward Cathy. She stopped and stood still once more.

"Lucky," shouted Chris. He fell backwards and to one side as Lucky's guns came to bear on him. Chris drew as he fell backwards and fired his gun. The bullet hit the bounty hunter in the chest. He staggered and fired both guns into the ground near Chris's feet. He then fell against one of the stalls then bounced to the ground. The sorrow horse quickly exited the barn.

"Chris," screamed Cathy as she ran forward. She expected to see him wounded, or dead. He was getting to his feet when she grabbed hold of him. "You hurt?" she asked.

"No," he replied.

"He didn't hit you?" she asked.

"Not a scratch," said Chris putting his gun back in the holster after reloading it.

She grabbed him around the neck and kissed his lips real hard. He put his arms around her and began to squeeze her closer. She pushed herself away and then she slapped him across the face with all her might.

"What was that for?" he asked rubbing his cheek.

"For scaring the hell out of me," she screamed and turned to hurry out of the barn. She was crying real loud all the way.

"What's going on in here?" yelled John as he came running into the barn. "This is no place to be shooting . . . take it outside!" He ran up to Chris who only pointed to the body lying in the nearby stall. "Who's that?"

"Lucky, or not so lucky . . . a member of the posse," said Chris. "He sent another one to tell the rest of them where to find me." Chris started toward the door.

"Where you going?" asked John.

"To get my horse," he said with out turning around "I'll lead them away so they won't cause you any trouble."

"I'll get the hands and we'll fight them off," said John.

"You'll only get them and yourself killed," said Chris as he mounted the horse John traded him. "I'll make sure they follow me." He pulled his new horse around and dug his spurs into the sides of the animal.

"Damn it all," said John. He stood looking at him riding away toward the high ground in front of the ranch's main gate. He reined up on the high ridge, there to wait for the posse to arrive. John ran to the bunk house and found Cookie fixing the noon meal. Where's all the men?" he asked.

"Their out on the range," said Cookie.

"Well get them in here right now," ordered John loudly. Cookie ran to the bell they used to call the hands to eat with. The cowboys all knew anytime they heard the bell ring and continued to ring, to drop everything and come running. Cookie pulled the rope and kept pulling it as the bell continued to ring. The cowboys were scattered across the ranch, but those who could hear the ringing of the bell left what they were doing and rode hard and fast toward the ranch house. John had his horse saddled and was now armed with pistol and rifle as the men came riding into the ranch compound.

"What's up?" said the men as they pulled their animals to a halt close to their boss. Five men had answered the bell.

"You all know Chris," said John "he's got some bounty hunters on his trail. He's gone to the high ground there to wait to lead them off so they won't bother us. He needs our help . . . anyone who wants to ride with me . . . arm your selves and let's ride."

In a short time all six men from the ranch rode out the main gate and up the gentle slope to where Chris was waiting.

"You should have stayed out of it," said Chris as John pulled up to his side.

"There's no way," said John.

"What are you trying to do . . . take on the whole world?" asked one of the cowboys.

"You fellows want to get killed?" asked Chris.

"We want in," said another cowboy "just in case there's more than you can handle, even if you did teach us how to defend ourselves."

"There could be more than you can handle," said Chris.

"The more the merrier," said another cowboy.

"I fought Indians and Mexican bandits before," said another "so bring on these green horns."

"All together now we make seven," said John.

"I like that number;" said Chris "could be, it's my lucky number."

They waited on the rise for nearly a half hour before the opposition rode into view. Chris counted the men riding toward them.

"Twenty five," said Chris "anyone want to pull out . . . now's the time."

"Hell . . . them fellows are vastly out numbered," said the cowboy on his right.

"You want them to go get more?" asked a cowboy on the left.

"Naw! I'll just have to shoot mine twice," he replied.

"Let's try to talk them out of a fight first," said Chris.

"And if they don't want to talk?"

"Then hunting season is open," said John.

The men rode up the rise and stopped about twenty yards away. In the lead was a tall lean man, dressed in black. He was packing a pair of Colts which he carried backwards in black holsters. He moved forwards a few feet and called out.

"Christopher Le Monte."

"That's me," said Chris and he moved a few feet forward and stopped.

"Your brothers want to give you your inheritance," he said "They're waiting in Odessa to meet with you."

"Did it take all of you to tell me that?"

"You keep dodging us," he said "we wanted to make sure you got the message."

"Okay . . . I got the message," said Chris "so you can all leave now."

"There is one more thing," said the man.

"What's that?"

"You're to accompany us to the meeting," he said.

Chris sat looking at the men in front of him. He was tempted to ride with them just to keep those behind him from getting hurt. But he knew that would not be wise on his part. Just then the men behind him came forward and stopped in line with him once again.

"You haven't forgotten about us, have you?" asked John.

"I don't want you to get hurt," said Chris.

"And we don't want you to get hurt either," said John.

"I don't want anything the Westons have to offer," Chris said "their not my brothers . . . my name is Le Monte and I am a Cajun."

The man in front of him said "That's too bad . . . they're real nice fellows . . . but have it your own way." He pulled his horse backwards into line with the others then he shouted "take 'em." Everyone on both sides drew weapons and began firing. Chris hit the talkative man and he went down. He fired his weapon until all the bullets were used, and then he drew his rifle to fire at anyone still in the saddle. Three men managed to escape and ride away. One of John's cowboys received a flesh wound to the arm. John sent him and one other ranch hand to get the Sheriff and to see the Doctor. The cowboys collected the horses and took them to the corral.

Cathy was waiting at the ranch house on the veranda when they rode back. She ran to meet Chris as he pulled his horse up to the hitching rail. They embraced when he dismounted. Their lips met in a long kiss as the cowboys hooted and hollered.

"That was some show," exclaimed Senator McWilliams.

"Well mother," said John as he climbed the steps to receive a hug and a kiss from his wife "Looks like we're going to have us a wedding."

"Maybe so," she said with a smile.

§

"What the hell is this nonsense?" screamed Phillip, as he wadded up the newspaper.

"What?" Bernie asked.

"It says that Christopher Le Monte and six other men fought off twenty six bandits near Willow Bend Texas with twenty four killed."

"Maybe Chris is among the dead, Phil," said Bernie with a smile.

"Wipe that grin off your face," roared Phillip "the bandits were the only ones killed. And don't call me Phil."

"Oh!" said Bernie in a low voice.

"How long I have waited to hear that he's dead," whined Phillip. "Why is it he keeps tormenting me so."

§

"Sheriff," said a man as he entered the office of the parish sheriff "we found another body."

"Another body."

"Yeah . . . it was right near that skeleton we found a few years back," he said.

"Oh! Yes the first wife of Colonel Weston," said the sheriff. "I'll get doc and we'll come right out. Just keep your men away from the area until we're all done."

"Doc's already out there, he was doing some fishing, so he's waiting for you."

"I'll get my horse and be right with you" he said as he put his hat on his head and started for the door.

§

"What do we have this time, Doc?" the Sheriff asked.

"You remember that lawyer who represented Christopher Le Monte?" asked the doctor.

"I believe I do," he said "he disappeared about the same time as the Le Monte boy."

"Well . . . he just reappeared again," said the Medical Examiner. "That's him there in the ditch."

"Can you tell me what killed him?" asked the Sheriff.

"Sure can . . . it was a large knife which penetrated his back just between his left shoulder blade and spine. I would say it may have even penetrated his heart. Either way he didn't live very long."

"You think the Le Monte boy could have done it?"

"No! Who ever it was, either was very strong, or he threw the knife with such force that it cut through the rib bones. No! I would say the Le Monte boy was not strong enough, nor was he capable of throwing a knife that hard. It was a full grown man who did it."

"The Weston brothers, perhaps?" asked the sheriff.

123

"Oh! No! . . . I'll leave that up to you," said the doctor "You'll have my report as soon as I can get to it."

"How about making it a priority, Doc?" asked the sheriff.

"I came out here to do some fishing and by gum that's exactly what I'm going to do. So you and that mad house of a parish can go jump in the river . . . only don't jump in the one I'm fishing in."

§

"Why are you being so bull headed?" Cathy yelled at Chris in the home of the Morgan's.

"We can't get married until I meet with my brothers and settle this thing once and for all," replied Chris.

"Daddy . . . can you reason with him?" she whined to her father.

"He's right . . . you two can't start life together with this thing unresolved," John said.

"Oh! you men . . . you're all the same," and she stomped out of the room.

"Now I know she's got a real temper," said Chris.

"She gets it from her mother," John smiled and then said "but she'll think about it for a while and finally she'll realize you're right."

"I sure hope so."

"You're going to meet with your brothers soon?"

"I want to settle this as soon as I can, so I'm going to send them a telegram.

Then we can meet anywhere they want."

"There's a telegraph office in Willow Bend," said John "I'll ride in with you right now." He took his hat from the hall tree and they stepped toward the door. John halted at the door to the veranda and called to his wife "We'll be back in a couple of hours."

§

Willow Bend was a busy place that day as the local ranchers and settlers went about doing their shopping. Wagons of all kinds were on the street, some laden with sacks of feed for the livestock. Some sacks contained food for the humans. Men and boys rode horses along the street, some going this way while others went the other way. Then there were horses tied to the hitching rails. People were walking in both directions on each side of the street while a few were crossing the street.

John and Chris walked their horses along the street and John spoke to those he knew, which was most of them. Chris smiled and returned the waves of the people who waved at them. They drew up to the hitching rail in front of a small building in the center of town. Over the sloping roof that covered the boardwalk was a sign that read 'Acme Shipping.' On the wall next to the door was a shingle with the word 'Telegraph' carved into the wood. They dismounted and walked into the office. John opened the door and waited while Chris entered first, and then he followed. Chris went to the counter and spoke to a little old man behind it.

"I'd like to send a telegram, Please."

"Sure you would . . . why else would you be here . . . I don't see any freight."

"I'll write it out," Chris took a pencil and a pad of paper lying on the counter and began to write.

"It won't do you any good," said the man. He stood to his feet and spit a long string of tobacco juice into a spittoon setting on the floor nearby.

"Why's that?" asked Chris.

"The lines are down," he replied. "They've been down for three days now."

"When will I be able to send my message?"

"What do I look like . . . a dad blame fortune teller or some other kind ah fool, how should I know?"

"What if I leave you the message . . . you can send it when the lines are back up and working again."

"Sounds reasonable," said the man. Chris finished writing the words on the pad of paper. He then tore off the first page and handed it to the man.

He read the words then looked up and said "That'll cost you one dollar." Chris reached into his pocket and pulled out a silver dollar. "Of course you could save your money . . . if you were to deliver the message yourself."

"How's that?" asked Chris.

The man spit once more. "You want the message sent to a Phillip Weston of Baton Rouge . . . don't you?"

"Yes, that's right."

"Phillip Weston was in here an hour ago . . . he wanted a message sent to a Bernie Weston in Odessa . . . and now he's waiting for the answer," said the man "You'll find him at the hotel . . . room 16."

"This is better then I could have imagined," said Chris.

"What was the message he wanted sent?" asked John.

"Mr. Morgan . . . you of all people should know I can't divulge that information."

"Either you tell me, or I'll take this place apart and you with it." John's words surprised Chris for John was a very mild mannered sort of a fellow.

"He says he found a man by the name of Christopher Le Monte." He blurted out the words with his hands raised to shoulder height.

"And?" said John loudly.

"This Bernie, he's to bring another man here so they can put an end to it . . . what ever it is?"

"Who's the man?" demanded John.

"He didn't say."

"We better go back to the ranch and wait for them to make the next move" suggested John.

"No! I think I'll go see Phillip . . . maybe I can end it right here and now," said Chris. He turned and walked out the door and into the street where he stood for a few seconds. When his eyes caught the hotel sign he started walking in that direction. John was unarmed so he went to the horses and with drew his rifle from the saddle scabbard. He then followed after Chris.

Inside the hotel Chris crossed the lobby and went to the desk. "If you want a room sir, I'm sorry to say we're all full up," said the desk clerk.

"No! I just want to speak to the ... person in room 16," said Chris, "Which way is it."

"That way," said the desk clerk pointing down the hall way on the ground level "all the way in the back."

Chris walked down the hall and stopped at the door to the room. He knocked gently and waited for a reply. After a few seconds, when no sound came from inside the room, he knocked a little louder.

"The gentleman is not in, sir," said a maid as she past by "he went riding this morning.   He does so every morning, and usually he's back about sundown."

"Thank you ma'am," said Chris as he tipped his hat.

"You want me to tell him you were here, sir?" she asked.

"No, ma'am," and he walked back to the lobby. John was standing in the doorway of the hotel. Chris crossed over to him.

"He's out riding; the maid said he'll be back around sundown."

"You going to wait for him?" asked John.

"No! That's more than six hours," he said "I'd rather spend the time with Cathy." John smiled and slapped Chris on the back as they walked along the board walk.

There came a report of a rifle shot which broke threw the air. Everyone on the street stopped where they were and looked for the source of the gunfire. Some of them even ran inside for protection. Chris drew his pistol and began to search the town for whoever had fired their weapon.

John called to Chris "I'm hit," and he fell to his knees onto the board walk. He was clutching his chest. "Betty," he gasped. Chris quickly cradled his friend in his arms and called his name "John ... John." His body shook then went limp. His shirt was soaked with blood as were his hands. Chris laid him on the boardwalk. He rose to his feet as the people began to gather around. "DAMN YOU PHILLIP," he screamed. His eyes quickly searched the buildings along the street for him or anyone who could have fired the fatal shot that took the life of his friend. A man came from inside the hotel with a blanket and covered John's body. Chris stood there searching for the villain. A man ran up the street and came to a halt near Chris.

"Drop the gun," he ordered with his ready for action.

"Go to hell," said Chris. His eyes narrowed and his right hand was tightly gripping his weapon. He was ready to put a bullet into the man if he was to try and stop him.

"I'm the law here," he shouted at Chris.

"Then you help me find who killed him," shouted Chris.

"Who shot him . . . if it wasn't you?" asked the lawman.

"Phillip Weston," said Chris.

"Marshal, it wasn't him that shot Mr. Morgan," said a woman standing next to the window of the hotel "the shot came from that window across the street there." She was pointing to the second story window in a building across the street. The sign on the front read 'Pecos Land and Cattle Company.'

Chris ran across the street and tried to open the front door. It was locked so he stepped back and raised his foot then kicked the door as hard as he could. The door splintered into several pieces.

"You can't do that!" the Marshal yelled as he came up behind Chris.

"I already did," he said as he entered the building. He proceeded carefully to go through the building searching for the gunman. The place was deserted as he could find no one on the main floor. He worked his way to the center of the building; there he found a stairway leading to the floor above. The Marshal came up behind him.

"This is my job," he said softly.

"I let one lawman take over once," said Chris "that fool got himself killed . . . that what you want . . . then go ahead."

"What is this all about?" asked the Marshal.

"Right now . . . it's about the death of my good friend John Morgan," Chris said in a sour tone. "So let me get on with it."

The Marshal pointed up the stairs and said "after you."

Chris took the steps slowly, with his back to the wall and his eyes on the railing above. He inched his way to the top. There was an office door standing wide open. He stood on one side of the door way and looked inside the room. When he could see that the room was devoid of anyone he moved to enter. He walked to the window which was on the front of the building. This was where the shot had been fired from, for on the floor was a spent cartridge casing. He pointed to the brass as the Marshal came to his side.

Chris turned to look back at the interior of the room. He went to a closet and opened it with a jerk and pointed his gun inside. It was full of all kinds of office supplies and coats, but no one was hiding there. He then went back to the stairs and proceeded to investigate each and ever office on that floor. He soon found that the building was indeed deserted except for him and the Marshal. Back on the street, John's body had been removed from the sidewalk and had been taken to the undertakers.

"Are you going to tell Mrs. Morgan?" asked the Marshal.

"I guess . . . I should." He mounted his horse and rode out of town toward the ranch. He held the stud to a slow gate and as he rode along he kept trying to find the right words to say to Betty and Cathy, but the words kept sticking in his throat. He wept as he rode along and his vision was blurred with the tears. About two miles out of town he came to the bridge that spanned the large ravine which cut across the country side. When he was mid span of the bridge a shot rang out to his left side and across the ravine behind him. The bullet struck him in the back and he fell forwards in the saddle. He kicked the horse and dropped the reins in one motion as he slumped forward. He gripped the saddle horn to stay aboard the animal. The horse instantly went into a full gallop as it hurried toward the ranch.

"Mama," shouted Cathy. She was standing on the veranda and looking toward the road and the gate to the ranch. Her mother came quickly to the door. "Mama, that looks like Chris's horse." She was all excited as she could see him hanging over the side of the horse.

Betty stepped out onto the porch. She looked toward the bunk-house, and then toward the barn. Two cowboys were working on a wagon near the large corral. "You men," she screamed "stop that horse." She then ran out into the yard as Cathy was running for Midnight to cut him off, but she was too late and the horse continued past her. "Chris" she shouted. One of the cowboys took his lasso and threw a loop over the horse as he sped past. The horse came quickly to a halt when he hit the end of the rope. The impact dragged the cowboy several feet forward. Chris fell from the horse onto the ground.

Cathy quickly knelt by his side and seeing the blood on his back screamed real loud. The cowboy with the rope took the horse into the corral, while the other one came to the aid of Chris and Cathy. He felt for a pulse to see if he was still alive.

"He's still in Texas," said the cowboy. Betty came rushing up to them. Cathy was cradling Chris in her arms and crying loudly.

"Let's get him into the house," shouted Betty. The cowboy pulled the couple apart and lifted Chris in his arms. Betty and Cathy took hold of each other as they followed the ranch hand as he carried Chris into the house. Another pair of cowboys was riding into the ranch compound about that time and they quickly went to help get Chris inside. "One of you, go get Doctor Corbin and hurry." A man ran to the corral and took a fresh horse and saddled it. He then rode toward Willow Bend as fast as the animal could run.

§

John Lucas Morgan was buried in the family cemetery sixty yards from the house. Almost every person in the county was in attendance. Betty and Cathy were dressed in black. Flowers were in great abundance around the little cemetery.

§

"You still with us?" asked the woman leaning over Chris. His eyes were blinking as he tried to shake the sleep away.

"Where . . ," he tried to speak. The dryness in his mouth and throat made any kind of speech very difficult.

"Where are you?" she said it for him. "You're in a room the doctor calls his hospital. It's just the spare bedroom of his house."

"Water," his raspy voice asked. She held up a cup for him and poured the liquid into his mouth very slowly, just a few drops at a time. He moved the droplets all around to moisten his parched mouth, and then he swallowed the water to relieve his throat. "Thank you," he said in a more normal voice.

"You're welcome," she said.

"How long have I been out?"

"It's been three days since you were shot."

"Where's Cathy?"

"Mrs. Morgan and her daughter said they don't want any thing more to do with you. That's why you're here at the doctor's and not at their ranch."

Chris suddenly felt like he had been shot again.

"You want anything else?" she asked "If not I'll be leaving. The doctor will be here in a few minutes." She waited for a response from him for a few seconds then when none came she left the room.

Bucky's words echoed through his mind "you have to be fast, accurate, willing to kill, and don't care if you die, if you die, if you die, if you die." The words echoed though his mind as the tears washed across his face and down into his ears as he lay on the bed.

131

"I don't care anymore."

§

"That blundering idiot," screamed Phillip. He was safely in his hotel room in Odessa when the Texas Ranger came to check on him. "He used my name at the hotel in Willow Bend."

"Did you hire him to kill this Christopher Le Monte," asked the Ranger.

"No! I only offered a reward to anyone to help me find him . . . he's my half brother . . . Bernie and I want to find him so we can share our father's estate with him . . . not kill him. I don't know who this fellow was."

"Then why did this fellow . . . whoever he is, try to kill Mr. Le Monte, but instead managed to kill Mr. John Morgan at Willow Bend?" asked the Ranger.

"I haven't the faintest idea," replied Phillip. "Maybe the fellow had an old grudge against this . . . John Morgan."

"Well there is no way it could have been you that fired those shots," said the Texas lawman "you couldn't have been in two places at the same time."

"Does that mean you're not going to hold me?"

"I don't see how, nor on what charge," said the officer "Only I wish you would go home and leave this matter up to us . . . oh, and no more rewards."

"I'll do that," said Phillip as he opened the door to the room so the Texas Ranger could leave "I'll be on the next train back to Baton Rouge tomorrow."

§

"Cathy," called the voice through her slightly open window at the ranch. It was in the early hours before dawn. "Cathy" he called the second time when she did not appear.

132

Soon she showed and threw open the curtains. "Chris," she raised the window to full open. "Chris, what are you doing here . . . we don't want any more to do with you." Her voice was firm as she scolded him.

"I came to see you one more time," he said with his hat in his hand. "I'm truly sorry about your father, but it was not my fault he was killed."

"Oh yes it is," her voice rose "if you had only taken off that gun, then none of this would have happened."

"What would that accomplish? Their out to kill me . . . if I take off my gun then I will not have a chance," he pleaded.

"You're a gunman and you'll be one until some one . . . (choke) kills you . . . so go away . . . we've suffered enough." She closed the window and drew the curtains to cover the glass.

He stood there for a few minutes hoping she would reappear once more. He finally turned and walked away toward the road where he had left his horse, Midnight. He stood by the fence near the gate to the ranch and waited until the dawn light came. He watched as the cowboys went about getting ready for the days work. When Cathy came out of the house he stood erect and strained his eyes to see her as she walked to the barn. Two or three minutes later she rode out through the open barn door. She then turned her horse toward the main gate. Chris mounted his stud and waited for her to come riding his way. She was at full gallop when she rode past him and reined her mount toward Willow Bend.

He spurred his horse and raced to catch up with her. She whipped her mare into a break neck pace to evade him. It was now apparent to him, she didn't want to see him, and so he pulled his horse to a halt. He continued to watch as she sped on down the road toward the little town. He then let his horse follow her at a slow lopping speed.

She was in Willow Bend a good ten minutes before he arrived. Among all the other horses and people he soon spied her. She was talking with the sheriff of the county. She stood pointing at him as he rode slowly up the street toward them. The sheriff came to meet with him in the middle of the street, as she hurried inside the jail house.

"Miss Morgan claims you're harassing her and her family," said the sheriff.

"I just wanted to talk to her and express my sorrow on the death of her father."

"She claims you tried to break into her house."

"No, I just called her to the window."

"If you go near her again . . . I'll have to place you under arrest," threatened the sheriff.

"That won't be necessary," he sighed "I'm leaving . . . for good," he pulled his horse in a one hundred and eighty degree turn and halted him for a few seconds. He looked over at the jail house, to see her standing in the door way. "Tell her. . ." he stopped.

After a few seconds the sheriff spoke. "Tell her what?"

"Tell her I'm truly sorry . . . and (choke) so long." He touched his stud in the ribs and the animal started a slow gallop down the street. He made the turn at the split in the road and headed north.

"He said he was truly sorry and so long," the sheriff repeated the message to Cathy. They both watched him ride away and out of sight. Tears were trickling down both cheeks on her face. "Goodbye . . . Chris," she sobbed.

§

"The sheriff of Willow Bend, says he rode north yesterday," said Bernie as he held out the telegram to Phillip. "Now where do you suppose he's headed?"

"I'll bet he's heading for Kansas City and the Bank Account," said Phillip. "That's our money and as soon as he gets his hands on it, we'll be there to collect it and give him what he has coming."

"We're going to Kansas City, Phil?" asked Bernie.

"That's right . . . so don't just stand there . . . get our bags packed. And don't call me Phil."

"They're still packed," whined Bernie "We just got home yesterday."

§

Marvin Lipton was at his desk in the Kansas City Bank. A cashier pointed to him, so the gentleman, dressed in black clothing could locate him. He came to stand in front of his desk.

"Mr. Lipton," said Chris.

"Yes," said Marvin rising from his chair. He held out his hand. "How may, I be of service to you, sir?" They shook hands and Marvin motioned to a chair. Chris seated himself and then spoke.

"My name is Le Monte . . . Christopher Le Monte . . . I understand you have been holding some funds in your bank for me."

"What is the name on the account?"

"Three names are on the account, Barbara Weston . . . Lucinda Le Monte . . . and Christopher Le Monte."

Marvin wrote the names on a pad of paper. "This will only take a few minutes, so please, make your self comfortable, and I'll be right back." He rose and walked to the long rows of filing cabinets behind the teller cages. There he looked through several drawers and finally removed a file. He read the inside documents then went quickly to the bank manager's office. He soon came out accompanied by the manager. Marvin came back to his desk; the manager motioned for the two bank guards to meet him at Marvin's desk.

"Is something wrong?" asked Chris, seeing the other three men approching.

"Not unless you're not who you say you are," said Marvin nervously.

"Do you have a weapon on you, Sir?" asked one of the guards.

"I do," replied Chris. "Is there a law against my carrying one?"

"Not unless you plan to use it," said the Guard.

"I have no such plan . . . I only came here to check on my account," said Chris.

"Can you prove who you are?" the bank manager asked.

"Not really . . . . Oh! yes there is . . . . The Lawyer Allen Jackson . . . he told me to use a seven sign code" Chris took a pen and Marvin handed him a sheet of paper. Chris thought for a few seconds then he drew an 'ï,' followed by an 'Ø,' then an 'π,' next an '◎,' then an 'μ,' to be followed by an '=', and finally by an '$.' He handed the paper over to Marvin who quickly looked inside the file and compared them to those on the instruction sheet.

"They match," said Marvin.

"I'm sorry if our precautions disturbed you in any way, Mr. Le Monte," said the bank manager as he held out his hand to Chris. He took it and they shook.

"Don't worry about it," said Chris. The manager waved the two guards away and he returned to his office.

"Well I guess this belongs to you then," said Marvin as he handed the file over to Chris. He took it and quickly looked though it.

"I don't understand," said Chris in a puzzled tone "Where's the money?"

"Oh! Well if you will read the last page there at the bottom."

"This is an address in Atchison," said Chris "I'm supposed to go there?"

"You have to go . . . or else you don't get the money," said Marvin. "I am instructed to give you the balance of the account. That's $50 and you're supposed to use it for travel expenses to Atchison."

"Who's behind this?" asked Chris.

"I only have the instruction contained in the file, and now you have it . . . so you now know all that I know about it. Sign this release and I'll get you your money."

"Okay . . . I guess I'll have to go on this . . . treasure hunt," said Chris.

"I told you he would turn up sooner, or later here in Kansas City," said Phillip to Bernie.

"Where is he?" asked Bernie.

"Our snitch, Marvin told me he was here yesterday . . ." Bernie cut him off.

"He's got the money and gone."

"Will you please not interrupt me when I'm trying to explain things to you," shouted Phillip.

"I'm sorry Phil," said Bernie with his chin on his chest.

"And don't call me Phil . . . my name is Phillip," he shouted.

"Okay," said Bernie in a low tone.

"Now . . . like I was saying . . . my informant, at the bank told me there was no money . . . not at their bank anyway."

"What happened to the $40,000 then?"

"Will you please, let me finish," yelled Phillip.

"I'm sorry, Phil . . . era Phillip."

"He has to go to Atchison to an address that was in the file," explained Phillip.

"Did you get the address?" Bernie asked with a smile on his face and his hands rubbing together.

Phillip held up a slip of paper and with a chuckle and said slyly "Naturally."

The address took Chris to a very fine mansion on a hill over looking the valley below, which was filled with all kinds of trains and rail lines. The huge house was surrounded by very neatly trimmed lawns and gardens. Flowers of all kinds were in full bloom. Their scent filled the air as he stepped from the horse drawn cabbie in front of the house. He stood and looked at the house for a few seconds.

"You sure this is the right address?" he asked the driver on top of the cabbie.

"Oh! Yes sir," replied the driver "I recognized it to be the home of Judge William T Manson, the very minute you told me where you wanted to go . . . You want I should wait for you sir?"

"If I'm not out in ten minutes . . . send in the cavalry to drag out my body."

"How's that Sir?" the puzzled driver asked.

"Never mind," said Chris as he past the driver a folded bill. "You may go."

"Thank you kindly sir," said the driver and he whipped up the horse and drove away.

Chris looked around once more then proceeded down the path to the huge double front door. He paused to check his clothing. He was dressed in a suit and ribbon tie with a lacy fronted white shirt. He stepped up to the door and lifted the knocker. He banged the knocker three times then took two steps back from the door. He was about to repeat the knocking when it opened to reveal a very young man, about the age of ten years, and very neatly dressed.

"You knocked, sir?" the lad asked.

"I was told to inquire at this address about an account at the Kansas City Bank," explained Chris.

"Well sir . . . in that case, it would be best if you were to inquire at the Bank in Kansas City, not in Atchison at the home of Judge William T Manson."

"They told me at the bank in Kansas City to come here and ask the Judge about the account," said Chris trying to get his point across to the lad.

"You wish to see my grandfather on a legal matter then?"

"That is precisely what I mean . . . is the Judge at home?"

"He's always home . . . now that he has retired," said the youngster as he stepped to one side and held the door open. "You may enter . . . but first wipe your feet . . . grandfather does not like people tracking dirt into the house."

"By all means," agreed Chris. He wiped his feet on the door mat and entered the foyer. The inside of the house was very ornate with rich raised panels made from the finest cuts of oak. Elaborate and delicate chairs and tables were placed about the room. Multicolored lamps were setting on the tables as were books and pictures. Chris waited for the youth to enter the room also, but looking around the boy was no where to be seen. "Hello," Chris called out in a low tone.

Soon an elderly man came into the foyer. "May I help you sir?" he asked.

"Judge Manson?" asked Chris.

"Yes," said the man "do I know you, sir?"

"My name is Le Monte . . . Christopher Le Monte."

"Ah! Yes! Mr. Le Monte . . . you're from Louisiana . . . near Baton Rouge, I believe" the Judge held out his hand and they shook. "My wife has been waiting several years to see you . . . please sir, come this way."

"There was a young boy here, but now he's disappeared."

"That's my grandson Carl, he likes to play the butler . . . you see today is Wilfred's day off. Carl used the hidden passage behind the panel to disappear . . . it leads to the servant's quarters in that direction." He turned and led the way down a long and wide hallway to a set of wide stairs. He slowly climbed the steps. Chris could see the old man was having difficulties in navigating the incline. At the top he took a sharp turn to his right and started down another hall that was very narrow. Three doors they past before the judge stopped in front to the fourth one. He knocked gently on the door. A woman in a nurse's uniform came to the door and opened it a little. "Is she awake?"

"Yes, sir," the nurse said and opened the door.

"My Dear . . . I brought someone to see you," he said gently.

"Who is it?" asked a woman with a weak voice.

"It's Christopher Le Monte, from Baton Rouge."

"Christopher . . . he's here . . . show him in," her voice rose to a higher level.

"You may enter sir," said the Judge.

Chris stepped into the interior of the room. It too, was very ornate and had very lovely furnishing. On the bed was a woman in a robe trimmed in fancy lace and she was in a setting position propped up by some pillows. He looked long at her face.

"Barbara," he exclaimed.

"You haven't forgotten me after all," she held out her arms to him. He came to her bed side and knelt to embrace her. "You used to call me Aunt Babs . . . remember."

"I remember . . . I thought you were dead," he said.

"I had to let everyone believe that I was," she said. Gregory Weston was going to kill me, so I ran away when he got drunk and past out. I hid out for several months and when I finally came out of hiding he was dead and you had disappeared."

"You left Robert behind."

"He was Gregory's son, so I thought he would be fine until I could find a way to get him away too. But I never counted on Phillip and Bernie taking over and turning him out the way they did. Father Andres knew where to reach me so he sent me a message."

"Where is Robert?"

"Hello Chris," the voice came from behind him. He turned and drew his S&W from his waist band. "Are you going kill me, too?"

"That depends on what you intend to do," said Chris.

Barbara took hold of his arm "Please Chris . . . put that away."

"My father killed your mother and you killed him," said Robert "I guess that sort of . . . . in a strange way, makes us even."

"Phillip and Bernie don't see it that way," said Chris.

"That's their problem . . . not mine," he said and took a step toward him with his hand out. "Maybe we're brothers . . . then again maybe we're not . . . however I have no feelings of resentment against you. We were once playmates and good friends . . . . Now I hope we can be . . . at least friends once more." He held out his hand. "The choice is yours."

Chris slipped the pistol back into his waist band. He stood looking at the faces of the three people in the room for a short while. Then taking the hand that was offered to him he said "Friends." Robert pulled him up tight and they embraced.

§

"Chris your train is about to leave," Robert said hastily. They were on the station platform in Atchison. Barbara, the Judge and Robert were there to say goodbye and see him on the train back to Texas.

"I wish you wouldn't go," Barbara said with eyes filled with tears "You could have a happy life here with us. The past three days have been a delightful time."

"Yes Chris, why don't you stay?" asked Robert.

"I want to see the west, the real west before it all fenced off," he said with a smile.

"Write me a line now and then," begged Barbara as she embraced him once more.

"Maybe I will," he said. She kissed him on the cheek. He felt the spot as she released him and then he walked to the train to step aboard. He stood on the platform and turned to wave goodbye to the trio waving to him. He yelled out "So long."

§

The cabbie pulled up in front of the ranch house near Kansas City and a well dressed man stepped out onto the driveway. He removed his baggage from the boot and handed the driver a folded bill. The driver gave him a sloppy salute and snapped the reins on the horses back and drove away.

"Mr. Le Monte," said a man coming from inside the house to greet him with his hand out. "I was hoping you'd forgotten all about us."

"No way," said Chris as he shook the offered hand. "How's my horse?"

"He's one fine animal . . . and he's just great," said the man "I suppose you want to see him?"

"I have to be going," he replied "the sooner the better."

"I guess there's no way I can talk you into selling that stud to me then?"

"No way, at all," Chris said proudly "I raised him from a colt when his mare was killed by a mountain lion."

"He's in the corral," the man pointed and they walked to the enclosure. "He was one mighty tired animal when you left him with me, but he's been eating really well and now he's just plain fat and sassy . . . he might just want to buck a little."

"I don't think he'll buck, but just incase," Chris took off his fancy hat and jacket.

"You can change in the tack room," said the man leading the way.

Soon Chris stepped out into the corral dressed in his black shirt, pants, boots, spurs and his black gun belt and Colt revolver. He placed the black hat with a silver studded hat band on his head and dropped the cord behind his head and down his back. He stepped toward the horse at the far end of the pen. Chris stopped in the center of the corral and whistled loudly. The horse turned his head toward him. He whinnied loud and long, and then he came trotting to him.

"Midnight, how have you been?" said Chris as he rubbed the horse's nose. The animal snorted and then whinnied once more. "Oh! So you want to go too." Chris walked to the fence where the ranch owner placed the saddle and tack. Chris placed the items on the horse and then stepped aboard for the ride. Midnight snorted then made a right turn as Chris gently neck reined him in that direction. He nudged him with his spurs to a slow trot around the corral for a few laps. Chris pulled him up at the gate. "Open it up."

The rancher removed the latch from the notch in the log post and swung the gate open. Chris rode out and pulled up to the doorway to the tack room in one corner of the barn. He dismounted and placed the reins on the fence. He then went inside and returned with his saddle bags and a sack of supplies. He tied them behind the saddle.

"You'll be, wanting this, too," said the rancher as he handed Chris a Winchester Rifle.

"Thanks for every thing," said Chris as he shook hands with the man. "Do I owe you anything more?"

"Not a cent," said the man "That is . . . maybe I should be paying you."

"What for?" asked Chris.

"My three mares ... they have been very friendly with your stud."

"I see ... well in that case I hope you will get some really good colts." He mounted once more and reined the stud toward the road way. "So long," Chris waved a sloppy salute and started to dig in his spurs.

"Hold it right there," said a man stepping through the big barn door from the interior of the barn. He held a short double barreled shotgun in his hands and it was pointed at the two of them.

"Phillip Weston ... where's Bernie?" Chris asked.

"I'm right here." Bernie stepped out through the barn door, too. He walked a few feet past Phillip. He also, was holding a shot gun with double barrels on the short side.

"It's good to finally see you again, Chris," said Phillip "Now at last we can even the score for our father,"

"If you intend to kill me with those shotguns then let me get off my horse and let the man take him out of the way."

"No such luck," said Phillip sharply "I'm going to count to three . . . then we're both going to fire off both barrels. You can draw anytime after that." He laughed a little and then Bernie joined him.

"Drop," said Chris very quietly to the man standing next to him and the horse. He looked up into Chris's face and he returned the glance. The rancher's face was white as a ghost.

"One," said Phillip and Bernie laughed with anticipation.

Chris repeated his word to the frightened man "drop." The stockman looked toward the pair with the shotguns. "Let me get the horse out of the way," pleaded Chris.

"Forget it," shouted Phillip.

"Two," said Phillip and Bernie both laughed wildly and looked at each other. Chris didn't wait any longer he kicked the man in front of him as he dismounted on top of him and drew his six gun. He fired as he fell to the ground. Phillip was hit in the chest and he staggered backwards and turned to his right. Bernie turned to see him falling to his knees. Bernie quickly retuned his eyes to search for Chris, but as he brought the shotgun back in Chris's direction he was stuck in the chest with a slug from the Colt in Chris's hand. He dropped the gun and fell onto his back. Phillip rose to his feet and then staggered as he raised his shotgun once more in Chris's direction. He looked at Chris and opened his mouth to speak, but fell forward to place the barrel of the shotgun in the dirt. His last act was to pull both triggers. The blast kicked him over backwards as the barrels exploded. Chris was struck with a few small pieces of shrapnel from the explosion with no damage to his person.

"You okay?" asked Chris as he went to the aid of the rancher.

"Yeah . . . I think so," he got to his feet. "They were going to kill us both."

"They've been after me for the past ten years," said Chris as he stepped toward the pair on the ground. He reloaded his gun and returned it to the holster.

The stockman went to inspect the bodies. "Hey, this fellow's still alive." He was kneeling beside Bernie.

Chris came to him and knelt down beside him. Blood was running onto the ground from the wound in his chest despite his attempts to hold it in with his hands. "I don't want to die," cried Bernie. His speech was ragged as he bled. "We killed that lawyer . . . . Allan . . . Jackson."

"Who else?" Chris asked.

"We hired a man . . . to kill you at . . . Willow Bend . . . but he missed . . . he killed (gasp) . . . another man."

"John Morgan."

"I guess so."

"What's the gunman's name?"

"Billy Reno," Bernie said with his voice fading fast. He released his hold on his chest and his body went limp.

"Where can I find him?" shouted Chris. He grasped the clothing and shook him.

"He can't hear you," said the rancher "he's dead."

"Billy Reno . . . . I'll find him if it's the last thing I ever do." Chris rose to his feet and walked to his horse. He mounted and let the animal walk up to the rancher "I'm sorry for the trouble . . . can you explain it to the law?"

"Don't worry about it," he raised his hand to Chris "Thanks for saving my life."

"So long," Chris said as he released the man's hand. He dug his spurs into the ribs of Midnight and they rode away at a slow trot out to the road leading south.

§

"Here's one for you Doc," said the sheriff as he came into the Parish Medical Examiners office. He handed the doctor a telegram.

"What's this?" He took the paper and read the message. "Well I'll be . . . Christopher Le Monte killed those two Weston Brothers.

"I think he saved the taxpayers of this parish the expense of another trial . . . don't you?" the Sheriff asked.

"It does in deed."

"The only thing I'm worried about . . . if he keeps it up I'll be out of a job." They both laughed.

§

Barbara and the Judge decided to take a trip to Philadelphia. For her it was to see some relatives, while it was a business venture for the judge that caused them to make the trip. They rode the train all the way. They were staying at the home of her Aunt Maud and Uncle Charles Marlstone. He was a member of the state legislature. To honor their guest they held a large party on the lawn of their very large estate just a few miles outside of Philadelphia. The place was swarming with guest and servants, while the younger set ran and played games about the grounds.

"Barbara . . . this is Miss Cathy Morgan . . . she's staying here with her Aunt Polly and we are hoping she'll make it permanent," Aunt Maud made the introduction.

"You're not the Cathy Morgan, from Willow Bend, Texas?" Barbara asked.

"Why . . . yes . . . how did you know?" All the women in the circle wanted to know how she could have possibly known about Cathy Morgan.

"I know a great deal about you my dear," she replied. "I was once married to Gregory Weston."

145

"Chris," she gasped.

"I think we should have a long talk together . . . in private." Barbara took her by the arm and gently took her to a safe distance from the group. In a secluded corner of a lovely garden of flowers they stood in the shade of a very large tree. "Now, my dear, what is it with you and Chris?"

"There's nothing more between us . . . its over."

"What kind of a lame brain do you have in your head?"

"I resent that . . . how dare you."

"Come off it missy . . . you love him . . . and he still loves you. I spent three days with him in my home; he poured out his heart and soul to me about you."

"What if that is true . . . he's a killer . . . how can I ever marry a man like that?"

"True . . . he's killed . . . but the law doesn't want to punish him for it."

"Still . . . I'm going to marry someone else."

"Your parents really spoiled you rotten didn't they . . . you want every thing neat and tidy . . . well missy the world is not like that. You destroyed Chris's life and now you're going to destroy another man's."

"It's for the best," Cathy said.

"For who, you?" Barbara said loudly "You know what I think . . . you're not good enough for Christopher Le Monte." She turned to walk back to the group.

The train pulled into Abilene, Texas and onto a siding. When it came to a halt one of the workmen opened the door to the stock car and yelled at the man sleeping on the pile of straw. "Hey, you . . . Abilene . . . it's as far as we go."

He removed his hat from his face. He narrowed his eyes for a few seconds, until they were accustomed to the bright afternoon sun. He rose from his bed of straw, and then stepped over to the horse penned at one end of the car. He opened the gate and taking the lead rope, he led the animal over to the big doorway in the side of the boxcar. He slipped the rope in a ring on the wall and proceeded to saddle the horse. When the workman came back by, he yelled out "how about a ramp for my horse."

"Don't have one . . . you'll have to make him jump." Then he went on his way.

"Well Midnight . . . old boy . . . it looks like we'll have to jump out." Chris said as he mounted. "Don't break a leg." The animal was nudged to the open door where he lowered his head and studied the situation for a few seconds, and then he lunged forward when Chris gently touched him with his spurs. They hit the ground, recovered nicely, and then traveled along at a slow trot. Chris reined him toward the engine a few cars ahead. He waved to the men in the cab as he rode by them, and they returned his wave. "Thanks." He spurred Midnight into a slow gallop as they continued into the town some distance away.

They rode along the dirt Main Street and past lots of false front buildings. There were a few people milling about the little town. He pulled Midnight up in front of a building with the sign 'General Store' across the front of the building. He tied the horse to the hitching post and went slowly inside. Several women were doing their shopping. The man behind the counter was busy with a pair of ladies showing some bolts of cloths from a pile on the counter.

Chris walked around to the area where the guns were in a rack. A woman came from the back and nearly bumped into him. "Excuse me," he said quickly and removed his hat.

"That's quite alright," she said "I should have looked where I was going. May I help you, Sir?"

"These ladies were here first," Chris said "I'll wait my turn."

"That could take all day," said an elderly woman nearby. "Millie you best take care of the young man . . . so he can go about his business." She turned and continued to scan the goods on one of the center tables.

"What can I do you for?" Millie asked.

"I'm riding south, so I'll need some coffee, beans, bacon . . . and some Colt forty-five ammo."

"One box?" she asked.

"Ten boxes . . . if you have that many?"

Everyone stopped what they were doing and looked at Chris.

"You going to a war?" asked the man who was helping the women with the cloth.

"No! I'll be on the trail for some time, so I don't want to run short."

"We don't get many gunmen in here," said the man coming over to Chris. "They mostly go to the gun shop."

"I'm no gunman," said Chris "just a man who wants to see the west."

"Who you running from?" asked the man as he touched Chris' arm.

"No! It's not like that," Chris pleaded "Really, I'm just a peaceful fellow."

"What's your handle?" asked the man.

"My name is Christopher Le Monte and I . . ." before he could finish all the women dropped what they were doing and fled the place.

"You killed those Weston Brothers in Kansas last week," said the man. He held out his hand "Pleased to meet you Mr. Le Monte."

Chris ignored his hand "Miss I need those supplies."

"Millie, get the gentleman his things." He with drew his hand.

She gathered up the items and put them into a cloth sack. She laid the sack on the counter and stepped back. The man placed the bullets into another cloth sack and handed it and the first sack to Chris.

"What do I owe you?" Chris asked as he took the sacks.

"Nothing," said the man.

"What do you normally charge other people for these items?"

"Ah ... well let me see ... ah ... $6 should cover it."

"I would normally have to pay $10 for this," Chris laid ten silver dollars on the counter "that about right?"

"Yes sir," said the man. "Thank you Mr. Le Monte."

Chris then turned and walked out to his horse. He placed the sacks into the saddle bags on the back of the saddle. Just as he finished a man with a double barrel shotgun came quickly up behind him.

"Don't try anything," he shouted "stand right there."

"What's this?" Chris asked.

"You holding up the store?" asked the man.

"No Marshal," said the shopkeeper stepping out onto the side walk. "He just came in for some supplies ... and he paid me."

"I was told a man was holding up the place," said the Marshal.

"Oh no, it was just a mistake. No one is holding us up," the shop-keeper reassured the Marshal as he lowered the shotgun.

"I was on my way out of town," said Chris "so if there's nothing you want with me, may I continue to ride."

"You're name Le Monte," asked the marshal.

"That's me."

"Well now, that was some gunfight you had with them two brothers in Kansas last week ... I'm a thinking maybe you'd like to set and jaw a spell."

Chris turned to face the man "nothing to tell ... two rats got them selves killed." He turned back and mounted the big stud. He dug in his spurs and said "So long."

§

Three days south of Abilene Texas, Chris came upon a small spot on the road. On one side sat an old house, corral, windmill and barn. Across the road was a building with the words 'saloon' painted over the door. He decided to take a break and have a few drinks. He pulled

Midnight up at the water through and tied him there. He stretched his limbs as he walked to the steps leading up to the sidewalk. He slowly stepped to the door and stood looking inside for a few minutes before entering.

Inside were four men and two women. One of the men was in one corner with the two women. A little man was behind the bar. The other two men were seated at a table near the bar at the far end of the building. They were sharing a bottle between them. Chris entered the room and walked slowly up to the bar.

"What'll ya have?" asked the barman.

"What do you have?" Chris asked.

"Beer, whiskey, and tequila," replied the man coming to place both hands on the bar in front of Chris. His clothes were dirty and he smelled like manure from a pig pen.

"Make it whiskey," said Chris and he placed a coin on the bar. The barman set a glass on the bar in front of him then took a bottle from the back bar. He then pulled the cork out with his teeth and poured the amber liquid into the glass. He returned the stopper to the bottle and replaced it to where it had been setting. Chris took the glass and tasted it. It was a crude form of slow poison in home made 'rot gut.' He then drank the entire glass full. It burned all the way down.

"You want a woman?" asked the man in the corner with the women.

"No," Chris said.

"You got something against women?" yelled the man.

"Not a thing."

"You know what I think . . . he's afraid of 'em." The man and the women laughed out loud and the barman snickered a bit.

"Could be," said Chris. He turned to leave.

"That's it . . . run before they bite you."

Chris glanced in his direction to see him rise to his feet and start toward him.

"I suppose you're a real mean hombre with that gun, too."

"Let it alone," said Chris. He removed the tie on his Colt.

"Don't draw Mister . . . that's Billy Reno . . . and he's real fast with a gun" cautioned the barman.

"So you're Billy Reno," said Chris as he went into his stance to draw. "I've heard about you."

"Is that right . . . what have you heard?" inquired Reno as he, too went into his favorite position to draw.

"Nothing good . . . everyone says how you like to shoot people in the back," said Chris.

"That's a lie . . . I never shot no one in the back," roared the man.

"How about John Morgan?" Chris watched his face "you remember Willow Bend; the Weston Brothers wanted you to shoot me."

"You're Christopher Le Monte," screamed the man as he went for his gun.

Chris and Billy both fired bullets at each other. The women ran screaming from the room. The barman ducked behind the bar for safety. The two men sharing a bottle kept on drinking, they only paused long enough to hold up their glasses in a salute to the winner.

As the smoke cleared, Billy lay dead on the floor. Chris was slumped into a chair as he held his left side. Blood ran down his shirt, onto his pants and then dripped to the floor. The barman came slowly out from behind the bar and looked long at Billy Reno on the floor.

"You got something to stop this bleeding?" moaned Chris.

"Sure thing, Mister Le Monte," He ran to the door and yelled out to the house across the road. "Bring that medicine kit." He came back to Chris. "You gonna live?"

"I'm trying real hard," said Chris though his gritted teeth. "Damn . . . it sure hurts like hell."

"The Misses, she's good at doctor-in' people . . . she'll have you fixed up in no time."

"You better send for the Law . . . that man's wanted."

"You after the reward?"

"No."

"Then why send for the law?"

"To let someone special know that the killer of John Morgan has paid for it."

"Who'd that be?"

"His daughter. . . Cathy Morgan."

§

Chris opened he's eyes and stared at the ceiling for a few seconds. The sculptured tins ceiling tiles were see you in a few days. The room was lit by several lamps hanging on the small buggy wheel dangling from the ceiling. He turned his head to look to his right and down the length of the room. He was near one end of the room. A woman dressed all in white was leaning over someone on a table, covered with a white cloth. Across the table from her was another woman, also dressed all in white. They were involved with the person on the table.

Chris tried to rise, but there was a very sharp pain in his left side and he let out a loud moan, "oowh."

The woman close to him turned to glance in his direction. "You better lie still, or you will bust some stitches, then you may bleed some more. You have lost just about all the blood you can spare. Any more and they'll fit you with a pine box."

He relaxed and felt the heavy bandages around his mid section with his hands. A few minutes past and then the two women came to his bed.

"How are you feeling?" inquired the woman taking his hand and feeling for his pulse.

"Rotten."

"Any pain?" she asked. Then she leaned over him and looked deep into his eyes.

"Yeah, my side hurts a lot."

"What kind of pain, aching, or sharp?"

"Aching" was the reply.

She reached over to the table nearby and removed a bottle of liquid. Taking a large spoon, she poured some of the contents into the utensil. She placed the bottle on the table and turned to Chris. "Open wide," she commanded. He complied and opened his mouth; she placed the spoon laden with the liquid between his lips, and then poured it into his mouth.

"Yuck," he shuddered. "That stuff is nasty, what is it?"

"Laudanum," she replied "it's a strong pain killer."

"That's opium," he said "and that's addictive."

"You want to hurt," she snapped "or do you want to rest and recover from your wound?"

"I was shot and just bleeding," he explained.

"That's right," she said "only the bullet hit an artery and you were close to bleeding to death when we came along."

"I thought the wife of the barman took care of me."

"They didn't have a clue as to the extent of your injuries. My husband and I took care of you after you past out. I operated and repaired the severed artery. Now, you need lots of rest and quiet."

"Your husband is a doctor?" Chris asked.

"Yes, only he's a Doctor of Divinity."

"Who's the doctor that patched me up?"

"I told you, I did, me, myself," she said very strongly in his face. "I am Katherine Wilson, a Certified Doctor of Medicine by the State of Texas."

"Where's my horse?"

"What? You were nearly killed and all you care about is your horse."

"Your husband is a preacher and you are a medical doctor," reasoned Chris slowly. "So I was thinking about riding to some place where the people are sane."

"Very funny," she said. "Just like two grown men seeing how many bullets it takes to kill each other."

"I'm sorry, I apologize, doctor," he said "Thank you very much."

"Well anyway you haven't lost your sense of humor." She adjusted the home made quilts that covered his body. "Warm enough?"

"I might be if you were to give me a tall glass of Bourbon," he chuckled.

"Water is what you need and lots of it."   She turned to leave the room.

§

"Well, how are you feeling today?" the tall man said when he approached the bed where Chris was snuggled up trying to keep warm. There was not much heat in the room, despite the pot bellied wood stove in the center of the room. The old building was so full of holes the wind could play a tune, as is whistled through each hole.

"I'm about half frozen," replied Chris. "My fever is the only warmth I have left."

"I'll see what's with the stove," said the man as he took a chair next to the bed where Chris was reclining. "I'm Doctor Justus T Wilson." He held out his hand. The men shook hands and Chris quickly returned his hand under the covers.

"Your wife did her scolding me yesterday," Chris said "so I guess it's your turn today."

"I don't want to scold you," said Doctor Wilson "I wanted to talk to you about the Lord Jesus."

"I was raised a Catholic," said Chris. "My mother used to read to me from the Bible at night."

"Well, that's a good start, but what have you done about the Son of God?" asked the Doctor.

"I am quite a few years too late to help him, or to get even with those who killed him."

"That is not what I meant; you see he died to save you and all of man kind who believe in him and the plan of salvation that he brought to us. Man is sinful and always will be, until each one repent and except his blood to wash away our sins. Then because he arose from the tomb we, who believe in him will have eternal life with him forever. When we accept the gift of pardon, we can then enjoy life and then work to serve our Heavenly Father."

"I heard that all before," said Chris in a huff. "It didn't help my grand parents. They died poor and were worked to death. Then my mother was raped and later she was beaten to death."

154

"Yeah, Chris, I know all about it," said Justus "then you turned to killing, first your father then anyone who was a threat to you. And now you were nearly killed, but we came along to save your life. The next time you may not be so lucky. Your brothers are now gone and so is Billy Reno, so who is left wanting to fight with you? Why don't you take off that gun and settle down and live like a real man? As long as you wear that gun you will always draw the bad ones to you."

"You could be right," Chris said slowly with deep thought.

Chris you're going to be in the care of my wife for a few weeks," he handed a Bible to him "I want you to read the book of John. Will you do that for me?"

"Are you taking care of my horse, Midnight?" Chris asked.

"You read the Bible and I will take good care of him." He extended his hand once more, and they shook. "I'll see you in a couple of days, I have to go and do some preaching in a nearby town." He walked over to the stove and poked it and placed another couple of chunks of wood into the fire chamber. "Rest and get well."

"So long . . . . Preacher."

§

"Aunt Polly I have to return home," said Cathy as she came into the room they called the Parlor. It was where her Aunt entertained her lady friends when they came too visit.

"Why Cathy dear . . . I thought you were going to stay here with us for all time."

"I just read this letter from a friend in Willow Bend," she said "The man who killed my father has been killed in a gunfight."

"That's good . . . serves the ruffian right . . . after all any one which lives by the sword shall perish by the sword." She was trying to quote the Bible.

"It was Chris he was fighting," she said with a sigh "he was wounded in the battle."

"Cathy, dear . . . you can't seriously be thinking about going back to that kind of a man? I mean after all he's killed so many . . . why only last month he killed those two men in Kansas. I guess his turn will come sooner or later."

"I have to go . . . I have to face him."

"You're making a very big mistake if you go back."

"I'll be making a bigger mistake . . . if I don't."

§

"Your name Le Monte?" a man asked Chris seated at a table in the hotel dining room in Odessa Texas having his morning meal.

"That's right Christopher Le Monte," he replied.

"I hear you're a pretty good gunman," said the elderly man.

"Gunfighter . . . not gunman," Chris pointed out.

"Whatever," said the man "I want someone to get rid of a mean nasty owl hoot by the name of Wilber McKing."

"You want me to shoot him?"

"Shoot him, drown him, throw him off a cliff, but get rid of the no good skunk."

"What makes you think I'll do it?"

"$500 says you will."

"Is that so?"

"Yep," said the fellow as he handed Chris a stack of silver dollars. "Here's $50 on account. You'll find the no good varmint out at his place just west of town about ten miles."

 "You want me to ride out there and do the fellow in . . . just like that?"

"Yep," he replied "and I want to watch you do it."

"You want to watch me do it?"

"Yep . . . he's been asking for it for a long time now."

"You want to show me where he lives?"

"Yep . . . that's so I can watch you do it."

"I'll get my horse and we'll ride out that way then."

§

"That's his place," said the elderly man as they rode up to the gate which stood wide open. They reined their horses through the gate and continued on toward the house. Chris rode right up to the house and they stepped down from the horses.

"McKing," Chris yelled real loud. A few moments later another elderly man came to the door of the house. He was holding an old single shot rifle in his hands. The weapon was the kind that had been used during the Civil War between the States. It was a muzzle loading kind that used a very large 'Mini Ball' type of bullet and black powder.

"You better say your prayers," shouted the first man.

"You get off my land," shouted McKing.

"Not until this feller shoots you full of holes."

"What is it between you two," asked Chris.

"That skunk fought for the Confederate Army," yelled the first man.

"That was my choice to make and I chose it," said McKing.

"So . . . he fought for the south," said Chris.

"He was suppose to fight for the Union, but oh no, he ran out on me and I had to serve in the Union Army."

"Wait a minute," yelled Chris "what has that got to do with anything."

"You dumb . . . or just plain stupid," barked the first man.

"Explain this to me, will you?"

"My name is Wilber McKing and I was living in Pennsylvania when the war broke out. I was called to serve in the Union Army. If I could find someone who'd take my place then I wouldn't have to serve. This rat said he would go in my place and I gave him $50 to take my place . . . only he doubled crossed me and went and joined the rebs."

"You're name is Wilber McKing . . . and your's is . . ." Chris pointied to the first man then to the other one.

"My name is Wilber McKing too," said the second man.

"You're both named Wilber McKing."

"That's right . . . we're cousins" said the second McKing.

"And that is what all this is about?"

"That's it," said the first McKing. "So I want this traitor shot full of holes."

"You and whose army is going to do that," yelled the second man as he rushed forward to face his cousin.

Chris quickly took the rifle from the hands of the second man and stepped back as the two began to yell in each others face. Chris inspected the weapon and saw a cap on the nipple, so he cocked the rifle and pulled the trigger with the barrel pointed skywards. The loud report of the weapon being fired sent them both ducking for cover. A thick blue-black cloud of smoke drifted slowly away.

"You promised to pay me $500 to shoot him . . . you gave me $50 so where is the rest of it?" Chris asked. He tossed the old gun aside.

The first elderly man pulled out his purse from his jeans and took out some gold coins. He counted out several $50 coins and handed them to Chris. "Now you going to shoot him full of holes?"

"Just a minute," said Chris as he turned to the second man "Now, you saw him pay me to shoot you."

"You dang right I did and I'll swear to it in a front of a judge, too."

"Will you pay me $500 to keep me from shooting you and shoot him?"

"You dang right I will," the second man pulled out his purse and counted out some gold coins. He handed the stack to Chris. "Now it's your turn to get shot full of lead."

"There's one thing you both have over looked."

"Yeah, what's that?" They both asked.

"I now have a contract from each of you to shoot the other . . . as I see it if I shoot you both . . . neither of you win . . . on the other hand if I keep half the money you both gave me and give each of you back half then the next one who causes trouble for the other one is the one I'll ride back here and shoot . . . is that agreed."

They both stood looking at each other for a few minutes than they both said "agreed."

"Good...here's your money," he handed them each $250 then mounted his horse. "Remember the first one who causes trouble for the other is the one I'm going to shoot full of holes."

They both stood in the yard as Chris rode away at a slow gallop.

"You think he means it?" asked one of them.

"I reckon he does fer shore?" said the other.

"It look's like the feud is over then."

"Yep, shore nuff."

"What'd he say as he rode away?"

"So long."

§

"Cathy you can't set out here all the time" said her mother Betty.

"I'm going to wait right here until he comes back," she said as she pulled the heavy blanket around her. It had been cold for several days and it looked like it might even snow.

"It's warmer inside by the fire," Betty said.

"He's out there somewhere ... and its cold where he's at ... so I'll wait right here."

"Alright ... I'll get you some hot chocolate to drink." The woman turned and walked back inside the house to go to the kitchen. She set the pot on the stove to boil the water. She looked around at the house which had been her home for nearly forty seven years. Some how, it looked old and barren with out her husband, John, there to help brighten it for her. Her thoughts of the good and bad times ran though her minds as she looked around. The whistle on the pot sounded off, but she was years away in remembrance of those days. Her mind at the moment was locked onto the little girl who was trying to walk across the floor as John held out his hands to catch her.

"You better take care of that before it all boils away," said a strong voice in the door way to the dining room. She looked up

159

into the face of Jane, a neighbor, who came to stay with her while Cathy was away. Jane was a little younger than her and she had a voice more like a man than a woman. She was a widow and lived by herself at the edge of town; she did odd jobs to survive. By moving in with Betty, life for both of them would be much easier.

"I was just making some hot chocolate for Cathy," said Betty.

"Let me do that before you boil away all the water," said Jane.

"Why don't you make enough for us all," said Betty as she took a seat at the dining table.

"She . . . still out there?"

"Yes . . . I'm afraid she'll never come in now." Betty placed her face into her hands and began to sob.

"It's been almost four months since we've heard anything about him," said Jane. "I wonder where he could be."

"John used to ask that ever sundown," Betty said "I'm hoping Chris is still alive, for Cathy's sake." She wiped at the tears on her face.

§

The night air was cold as Chris rode into a small town near the banks of the Pecos River. He pulled up at the Livery Stable and dismounted. He stretched his legs to regain his full use of them, and then knocked on the office door. A man was leaning a chair back against the wall reading a newspaper. He looked up through the window to see the stranger standing just outside. He quickly went to the door and opened it.

"You got a stall for my horse?" Chris asked.

"Fifty Cents for the night and all the hay your horse can eat," said the stable master.

"How about some oats?" Chris asked.

"Two bitts more," he said.

"Okay," he gave the man the money. He then removed his saddlebags and rifle.   "Where's the hotel?"

"Don't have one . . . it burned down last month," he said "if you want a room . . . the saloon might have one . . . or you could sleep up in the hay loft . . . it's free." The man said as he pointed upwards with his thumb.

"I'm frozen to the bone," said Chris "so I'll try at the saloon." He patted his horse, Midnight on the rump and turned toward the row of buildings across the street. The building on the far end was the only one with saloon painted on a sign which hung over the doors. He hurried to escape the cold wind. He opened the outer doors, the batwings were tied back. He went inside the saloon, closed the door and stood just inside the door way for a few moments. He looked around to read the room once over. The only people in the room were three men, seated at table playing cards. A woman was standing behind one of those playing cards. Another man was behind the bar. Chris walked up to the bar. "I'm looking for a room for the night."

"I got one," said the barman "but it's gonna be busy in a few minutes." He pointed toward the card game. "They're playing for the lady."

"Give me a shot of Bourbon then," he flipped a coin on the bar.

The barman took a bottle from under the bar. He set a glass in front of Chris and poured it full. He then set the bottle back under the bar. Chris lifted the glass to his lips and smelled the tantalizing aroma. The sights and sounds of the past began to rush through his mind of that day so long ago. His left hand gripped the edge of the bar for a few seconds. Chris sipped the drink to get the taste then he gulped it all down.

"Another," asked the barman. Chris nodded his head in the affirmative. The barman took the bottle and poured him another glass full. Chris had just placed the glass to his lips when he felt some hands on his shoulders. He looked into the mirror behind the bar. The woman standing close behind him was rubbing his back and arms.

"You're kind ah cute," she said in a soft voice. "Why don't you get in the game too?" She was wearing heavy make up to cover the wrinkles and discolored complexion from living in saloons and other places of the night. She also smelled of tobacco and whiskey.

"Damn you Nora," yelled the man she had been leaning on when Chris entered. "Get your tail back over here."

"You better get in the game, honey," she said as she walked away from him. "You might . . . just get lucky."

"No thanks," Chris said as he watched her twist her body as she walked. It was meant to attract his attention and to arouse him.

"What's the matter," she stopped and turned to face him "ain't I good enough for you?" she hissed.

"I should say not," said Chris with a grin.

"Why you," she came forward to take a swing at him which he ducked. When she tried to swing again he blocked it and she let out a yell "Oww."

The man she had been leaning on and had called her by name got up from the table and came rushing forward.

"Keep your hands off my woman," he yelled.

Chris could see he was wearing a pair of Colts. And by his stance it was plain to see that he meant to use them.

"Tell her to keep away from me," demanded Chris as he tried to block another of her swings.

"Nora get away from him," he yelled "I'll take care of him."

"Whoa up there fellow . . . I just came in to get a room and a drink . . . I'm not looking for trouble." He removed the tie on his side arm.

"You just found trouble," he growled "you can't treat my woman like that."

"Don't go for your gun," Chris cautioned "I can kill you, but I don't want to."

"Who the hell do you think you are, Christopher Le Monte?" bellowed the man.

"That's right . . . I am Christopher Le Monte," sighed Chris.

"How do I know you're really Le Monte?" asked the man nervously.

"If you pull that gun . . . St Peter will be vouching for me . . . . Or you can believe it to be true . . . and keep on living."

"He's lying," she screamed at him "he's a coward and just wants out."

"I say you're lying," said the man.

"Don't be a fool . . . I'm Le Monte." Chris watched the man's face as he waited for him to make the next move.

"You can take him baby," she shouted loudly "go get him."

The man's eyes narrowed and his lips parted to expose his clenched teeth. He swung his right hand in an upward movement and drew the sixgun from the holster. Chris beat him to the draw and fired the first shot. The man staggered as he fired, and his bullet hit the bar beside Chris. Then he grabbed his chest as he stood there his face covered with disbelief as his life oozed away.

"Baby," she came running toward him with out stretched arms.

"It's him," he moaned and raised the gun to fire again, only she stepped in front of his gun as she reached out to grab him. With the next shot from his weapon she fell dead into him and they both fell to the floor.

Chris looked around the room, but no one presented any threat.

"That was his fault," said the bartender "he pushed you into it."

"Damn it all," said one of the men who had been playing cards "I had a full house Aces over Kings."

Chris reloaded his gun and placed it back in the holster. "You got a lawman in this town?"

"No. The nearest lawman is a two day ride from here," said the bartender.

"I'll sleep in the livery tonight."

"That room is vacant now," he said.

"No thanks," said Chris as he walked toward the door he remembered the Preacher man's words, "they're all gone so take off the gun and live a normal life."

He turned and paused for a few seconds, he then said "So long."

§

Chris rode south and west for several days. He soon found himself on the ridge over looking the ranch of the Morgan's. He pulled his stud to a halt on the very top of the high ground. This was the very spot where the seven had fought off the twenty-five gunmen more than three years ago. In the early hours of the morning he could see the ranch compound. There was smoke rising from the chimney in the main house and the bunk house. He sat and watched as two cowboys left the bunkhouse. They went to the barn to get their mounts and ride out to the range west of the compound. He shivered in the cold gust of wind that blew past him, but he sat and waited. For the next hour he waited on the ridge. His attention was heightened when he saw a woman leave the house and hurry to the chicken pen. She quickly disappeared inside the hen house. He could tell she wasn't the one he was trying to see again. He was filled with a burning desire to see Cathy just one more time, even if it was only from a distance. However he was remembering how she had yelled at him to leave her alone. He wanted to ride down and tell her how he felt about her, but she had insisted that he not trouble them anymore. His heart burned all the more as he waited, for just one more look at Cathy.

As the sun was hidden behind the heavily overcast sky it was not getting any warmer. Then too, Midnight wanted to move on. He gently touched his spurs to the horse's ribs and they rode slowly down the gentle sloping ground toward the road leading into Willow

Bend. He rode at a slow trot as he went. Chris wanted to turn into the gate and ride toward the house, but fought off the temptation to do so.

§

Jane had gone out to the chicken pen that morning to feed them and collect the eggs. She was returning to the house when she spotted the lone horseman setting on the high ground just east of the house. She went to the bunk house door on her way to the main house and opened the door to the kitchen area. Cookie was cleaning up the morning dishes.

"There's some one on the high ground," she said to Cookie.

"Is that so," said Cookie coming to the open door. She pointed toward the figure who was now riding down toward the rode way to town. "I wonder who . . . by golly it's him."

"Who?" She asked.

"It's Chris," he shouted as he removed his apron and ran out into the yard waving it over his head. Chris was now out of sight beyond the ranch house.

"Miss Cathy," Jane screamed as she ran for the house. In the excitement she dropped the basket of eggs. "Miss Cathy," she kept repeatedly screaming as she ran forward.

Betty appeared at the door to the house to see what all the commotion was about.

"It's him," shouted Cookie as he ran past the house.

"Miss Cathy," shouted Jane as she reached the steps all out of breath "get Miss Cathy." She pointed up the road as Cookie ran in that direction.

Betty looked toward the road to see the lone figure riding toward Willow Bend. He was not looking back as he rode along at a slow pace. "It can't be . . . . by thunder it is . . . Cathy," she screamed as she entered the house "Cathy," she yelled in the front room.

165

"Cathy," she repeated as she climbed the stairs. At the top of the stairs Cathy came to investigate all the hollering.

"Mama what is it?" she yelled back. She was filled with dread that something was terribly wrong.

"It's Chris," her mother said.

"Chris . . . where?"

"Out on the road," Cathy pushed past her mother and ran for the door "Cathy it cold out there . . . put your coat on." It was no use to yell any more for her daughter, only dressed in her pajamas and bare feet, was now racing toward the road way. Betty grabbed the girls coat and began to race after her. The girl was running up the drive toward the main road so fast, there was no way anyone could possibly catch her.

The wind was blowing and howling about the country side, so their cries could not reach Chris's ears. He rode slowly and all the wile he wanted to turn around and go back. He ached terribly inside as he fought his emotions to go back.

Betty caught up to the aged Cookie who was leaning against a fence post trying to get his breath back. "Take a horse and go catch him."

"There're . . . all out . . . on the . . . range," he said as he huffed and puffed.

"Then ring the bell," she shouted.

"The . . . (huff) rope is . . . (puff) broke."

"He's getting away," said Betty "where are those two hands?"

"Out . . . (whew) on the . . . (puff) range."

"Maybe he'll stop in town," said Betty as she watched her daughter running past the gate and turning onto the main road.

There came the sound of a shotgun blast from the front of the house. They turned to see Jane laying on the ground with the weapon pointed straight up into the air. She had fired not one, but both barrels at the same time. The blast sent the woman backwards to fall over something witch tripped her. They watched as she tried to rise once more. Then they looked back toward Chris.

He faintly heard the shot in the moaning wind. At first he thought it was his imagination, but he looked back for a second to see a figure, scantly dressed running up the road over a quarter of a mile back. "What kind of nut is this?" he asked himself out loud. He pulled Midnight around to get a better look.

Through the howls of wind he thought he heard his name being called. He didn't know if it was real or not. Then as the figure drew nearer he heard his name once more. This time he knew who the 'Nut' was. He kicked the horse in the ribs hard and rode back at full speed, to meet the figure racing to catch up to him. He stepped out of the saddle twenty feet before he reach her. The horse ran past her and then came to a halt and turn back toward his master. The pair flew into each others arms to kiss deeply and emotionally.

"I'm sorry Chris," she blubbered when their lips parted. "I love you."

"I love you, too," he said and they kissed again and again.

"Don't ever leave me again," she cried into his chest as he held her close.

"Never again," he said. He pushed her back to arms length. "You make a habit of chasing after men in those things?"

"Only my man," she said and they embraced once more. She began to shiver from the cold as the extra warmth of her lengthy sprint began to leave her body. He took the blanket he had been using to keep the wind off his legs and wrapped her with it. He then placed her upon his horse, Midnight, and then mounted behind her. Together they rode back to the house as everyone went to greet them.

The End

The preceding was brought to you by Acme Saddle Soap used exclusively by the ranch hands of the Morgan Ranch. It protects the saddles from the BS that comes in contact with the cowboys.

Revised 20thAugust 2006 5:58 P M

Revised 6th January 2017 5:05 P M

Revised 13th January 2017 9:30 PM

Revised 3rd June 2018 1:02 PM

Revised 22nd September, 2018 11:45 PM

Revised 27th September, 2018 10:31 PM

Revised 18th October 2018 1:30 PM

Revised 20th October2018 7:33 PM

Revised 8th March 2019 4:18 PM

Revised 9th March 2019 4:43 PM

Revised 28th March 2019 12:08 PM

Revised 29th March 2019 5:24 PM

Revised 23rd April 2019 4:00 PM

Revised 10th November 2019 8:30 PM

Revised 3rd December 2019 2:40 PM

Revised 28th January 2020 12:19 AM

Revised 29th January 2020 11:42 AM

Revised 9th March 2020 2:48 AM

Revised 30th October 2020 4:05 PM

Revised 13th November 2020 5:32 PM

Revised 14th November 2020 5:29 PM

Revised 17th November 2020 2:15 PM

Revised 2nd December 2020 11:40 AM